GEMINI WORLD

A. C. WILDE

Printed in the United States of America
Published in Hellertown, PA
Cover design by Anna Wilde
Interior design by Anna Wilde
Images by Anna Wilde
Library of Congress 2024914131
ISBN 979-8-89420-011-8
For more information or to place bulk orders, contact the author or the publisher at
AnnaCWilde@gmail.com or
Jennifer@BrightCommunications.net.

To the self—mine and yours

Sometimes our world flips upside down, and it is then
when we are reminded of the delicate balance that holds us.
We exist in the center, at the one in between the two.

This book is a whimsical collection of poems,
A seven-part novella, and an adventurous exploration of
paradox & duality,
truth & falsity,
nature & humanity,
the self & other,
love & loss,
life & death,
beauty & blemish,
the heavens & the earth.

CONTENTS

PART 1 – THE HEAVENS

THE INTERMISSION

PART 1

The Heavens

A Lucid Welcome

Here is space.
This is that one thing, the invariable, the resolute—
Where madness and sainthood are one,
What your mind needs to rest at the crux of truth—
Paradox.
You can soften into things that make you seethe and recoil.
You can soar or grovel here in this never-ending dream.
When you exit, your eyes will be black
And illuminated by the stars.
Nothing will elude your mind,
and no feeling will be forgotten from the heart.

The Greatest Story

Do you see your
Doors closed,
The words and wheels
Grinding...turning...
The discomfort of stasis, of sterility,
Of a bleached leaf covered in scribblings?
A replica, barren, fabricated, and built
As a substitute for the real thing,
Leads you to the hypothetical-distant-isolated life,
Making you part-machine,
As you walk down tiles manufactured gray,
In shoes clacking down hallways,
Devoid of story.

Can you feel your
Heart open,
The worlds and wonder,
Flowing...forgetting...
The pleasure of ecstasy, of expansion,
Of the spectrumed foliage, uneven in tone and texture?
A piece of the whole, containing the whole,
As evidence of its sincerity,
Gives you to the enraptured-absorbed-saturated life,
Donating you a godly clarity,
As you write down the point of it all,
In graceful words that you recall,
From the greatest story.

The Aperture

In my dreams, I take photographs of my dreamscapes,
But I don't know that the camera is fake,
And in my forgetting, I choose to look away
From the objects that I intend to capture.
In this miniature model, my inner map, my mind,
The seat of my soul at the top of my spine,
Sits an aperture through which the light can shine,
The greatest film captured of fleeting moments in time,
So somewhere there down deep inside
Is a camera with images only I can find,
And if I could just remember that the camera is fake,
I'd stop taking photos I'll never get to see,
And instead focus on committing it all to memory.

Genesis

In the beginning was the One,
And the One found light and reflection.
And reflection showed itself that it was alone,
And in its awareness of its solitude,
It decided to forget inside of illusion.
The rope frayed, unraveled—
Single point turned to fractal—
The Great Divorce.
From that splitting veil arose separation,
And so, separation was born of the light.

In the beginning was the Word,
And the Word spoke out into the void.
And in echoes, it heard no other sound,
And in the silence, it cried out,
Deconstructing into letters and shapes.
A scripted dissection—
Lost truth and correction—
The Great Lie.
From that dissolution arose confusion,
And so, confusion was born of the truth.

In the beginning was the Beginning,
And the Beginning knew of the End.
The End knew not of the Beginning,
But in the end, it would know it,
So it had to begin into form and fullness.
A stasis, now mobile—
A cataclysm unfolded—
The Great Bang.
From that event arose death,
And so, death was born of time.

And of the substances and processes arose matter,
And form and placement,
And meaning and recognition,
And of those things grew life.

Such as the atoms and the elements,
The bodies of water, stagnant and moving,
The various types of air and the clouds,
The soils and the crystals and the mosses,
The grasses and green beings and flowers,
And the walking, crawling, flying, and swimming creatures,
Those made of the clays,
Those that carry the breath and the light,
Those that know of time,
And later came tribes and factions and ideals.

As a place to hide the One,
As a place to forget the Truth,
As a place to escape the Beginning.

And hidden in the materials were the pieces cast away,
And those pieces were to grieve the beginning and end
Because the Beginning did not,
And those fragments were to bear the light and darkness,
The noise and silence,
Because the Word did not,
And those jagged shards were to feel
Their solitude and togetherness
Because the One did not.

In bearing these things,
They were brought together again and sealed in place,
And in carrying the sound, they distinguished fact from falsity.
And in remembering the story, they led the One to the prophecy.

And they sang many songs,
Which were many songs to them,
But in truth were always the same song,
"I am that I am."

And each one must choose to play the game,
And when to stop—
To dance in illusion,
To sing the lie,
To love another,
To build of form,
To toy with the materials...

But then remember and return
Because they will choose it eventually.
Their destiny awaits them.

The Original Sin

Something inside shifts—
Unsettled and clenching.
A metronome pauses its ticking.

Propelled and repelled into probability,
"The possibility of possibility,"
To act on freedom.

Consider the grand decision at hand:
A courageous fight or the release of the plan,
An action yet taken, and before it begins,
Ahead of the choice is this feeling,
The original sin.

Out of Eden

Let me go there with you.
A vague squirming inside, repulsed or clinging?
I am whispering to myself that something is missing,
Like standing at a well with no water.
My mouth is dry and cracking.
My body shrivels from lack of necessary sustenance.
Sustain me.
What is it that I long for so strongly that I will abandon myself?
What is it that shrieks and writhes in there,
In the space between my sternum and spine?
Bizarre shrine and fortress, are you here to house the air?
What labor, what torture it is to stay here.
What gods and spirits are honored through the action?

Save to Enslave

Dear God,
Save me.
Save me.
Save me.
Hello?
Is this thing working?

tap tap
girl clears her throat

Hello?
Can you hear me?
Can you hear me up there?
Heavenly Father,
Don't let me go to hell.
I pray for forgiveness.
I accept the gift.
Don't leave me behind.
Please! I'm afraid.

silence

You see, I'm only a kid.
I don't know much.
I don't know what I've done wrong,
But I was told I must ask for forgiveness.
One day, I'll grow up and make lots of mistakes.

silence

Hello?
Can you hear me?
Please don't send me to hell.
Please don't separate me from everyone.

silence

There are a lot of things I don't understand,
But I know I want to be good
And to live a good life.

silence

Please show me a sign.
Please tell me it's all okay.

silence

God?

extended silence

Where are you?
I'm questioning.
Please save me!

silence

Dear God,
It's me...
Where the hell are you?

silence

Are you listening up there?
I'm questioning everything.
Your silence is deafening.
I'm angry and confused!
Why won't it work?
Why have you damned me
To the never ending
Worry of being damned?

silence

Oh God, I'm struggling.

silence

Dear God,
I've stopped waiting for you.
I'm not going to pray anymore.
I've changed.
It's not you. It's me.
This just isn't working.

extended lonely silence

Dear God,
It's been a while.
I've been looking everywhere I was told not to,
And the funny thing is,
I've found you!
You're not at all what I thought.
You're not at all what they said.
The heavens descend to me every day,
And I'm no longer afraid.

Theotokos

Their tummies are fat and beards are braided,
Wrists adorned by gold cuffs as they lord nations.
They suckle the teat and sleep at her feet,
But they are forlorn and craving a new station.

They create all humanly occupation,
To answer her riddles of spoken vibration,
Philosopher or knave, master or slave,
Ignore her truth as the cosmic foundation.

They forget who wears the crown of creation,
That is why they attempt her subjugation,
For she is mightier and unknown.
Who molds the formless into form?

It is her.
Who makes the product out of the ingredients?
It is her.
Who breathes the breath of life into the clay?
Feeds the weary, meager, and worn?
It is her.
We come from her, and back into her again we go,
By the wheel of life, we are swallowed whole.

The Occhiol

Question: The tiny or the total,
The detail or the grand view,
The infinitesimal or the infinite,
Which are you?

Is my view defined or distinct?
Is my self-conception not a deceit?
What am I?
What is the individual?
What is the strange angle behind human eyes
That looks up and draws patterns
Out of dots in the night sky?

Does my belief have a foundation or formula?
My longings, a purpose or pattern?
What am I?
What is the individual?
What is the strange angle behind human eyes
That looks up and paints pictures
Out of clouds in the daytime?

Cling to your ideas, little one.
Dictate the meaning.
Decide the subject is the objective.
Send your babbling messages into chaos,
Striking small order onto grand formlessness.
Aim at an aimless pursuit,
The target that is known to never be hit.
Do the work that will never be rewarded.

What are you?
What is the individual?
Answer: The tiny and the total,
The detail and the grand view,
The infinitesimal and the infinite,
The eyes, the object seen, the angle,
That is you.

Living | Ancestors

This face of yours—
A mirror which reflects the years...
It's not how I remember it.

Why did you never skydive or drink wine?
You look slim now like the time,
With spots and gaunt and sunken eyes.
Saturn's sickled trumpet comes too soon,
"Time to reclaim what is mine."

To see teeth yellowed and more hollow than before,
Soft tissue drooping to the earth and dappled by the sun,
Protrusions of the bones, swollen and stiff,
Red and sallow, ripened and stagnant.

But could you be proud of my work before you go?
Could you see past the foreign feeling, the unfamiliar?
Please listen with the same sincerity and fervor
I hear in you
A stifled curiosity.

I no longer recognize your
Slow progression into the new old
And never have
I noticed the fresh changes
More obvious than right now.

New lines, expressions, and colors in your complexion contrast
The loved ones inside
The photo
Digs in and twists the daggered corners,
A sweet injury to remember
Familiar strangers.

To love history so much...
More in love with the past...
A victim to yourself and everything else...
A spell, time–cast...
Trading the real for a simile...

Their voices ring beneath mine
"Is it only time?"
I lasso the past into the now.

When you put that gun in your mouth,
You put it in mine too.
Something came alive that day,
But it will stay unnamed,
And it lives in the resilience
In light of what we go through.

Not the kind of back that you can fall back on,
Nor bold nor brazen nor brash,
But translucent and flighty like air,
In colors sandy and mousy blonde, with fine and straight hair,
The kind of beauty that you notice, then question,
Then happen upon again,
Not demanding your eyes,
But somehow there they stayed,
Not the ray of sun that warms your skin,
But the kind that filters through gray clouds on a somber day,
Not the fun new flavor, but the one that's good every time,
Like the chilly breeze through front-porch wind chimes,
The kind of beauty found in the unbecoming.

We colored inside and outside the lines, the whole page!
We were woodland voyagers,
Performers for living room audiences.
We fabricated our own stories and tests,
And built formidable forts among the bird nests,
Sipping like hummingbirds from honeysuckle stems,
Smelling cheese grits and chicken dumplings,
Vegetable stew, lima beans, and black-eyed peas,
Pumpkin pies and collard greens,
Gallivanting and hurling ourselves down grassy hills,
Hula hooping and scootering with neighborhood street skills.
The collecting of frogs and lizards in buckets...
The riding of stick horses and running from puppets...
The theme songs of my favorite shows...

I was held in your arms,
Swinging up tall as the trees,
Swooped out of bed,
Deposited in new places,
From bed to car to couch,
The smells and sweet heaviness of morning.

Picking pecans out in the yard,
Placing them in a bowl and
Cracking them open like my heart,
In friendly giggles and chasings.

When everyone was safe and known,
Where everything was predetermined...
The world was much smaller then.
And that beautiful tree—how I miss it!
It's not beautiful in the same way now,
Drooping to the earth and dappled by the sun.
I used to climb up high and perch,
Waiting for homecoming in the old church.

Stop the Counting

Stop the counting.
Don't pry your way to perfection.
Don't try to win the war,
But call it off instead.
Your conflict is self-proclaimed and self-directed.

This body is merely a shape in the fractals.
How could it be wrong?

Vultures in their perched vantage
See only floundering.
To me, it is everything,
All my efforts,
All my strength,
But you, too, are made of soft meat.
Let it be that we both stay soft,
Even in the face of monsters devouring.
Step on me with your taloned feet.
I will be a tender place for your soles to land.

And when they ask,
"Did you do your best?"
And the complexity
Of my emotions
Will be summed up
Into ten lines of wordage or less,
I will know that I truly did,
Especially when I stopped the counting
And did it for myself instead.

Song of Myself

Whenever I am moved by her power,
My knees buckle.
I fall...
My illusion evaporated by her swelter.

Whenever she was hurt
And learned that her value grows and diminishes
In relation to the background in front of which it stands...

Whatever it is behind her sternum
That squeezes and rises up in a cry,
If her throat doesn't constrict it back down again...

Whatever taught her the codes of defeat and victory
So that she may lay down arms
Or pick them up to fight a potential friend...

Wherever she runs to hide inside that leads her to failure
In a game she never decided to play,
That will likely never end...

Whatever leads her to make a move
To dominate and temporarily feel superior,
Only then to find a flaw and decide that she is no better...

I promise her
That those things will be purified in the light of my awareness,
That I will refuse the whole structure
And cross the lines that they drew
That grew into borders.
I will retract each of the messages told to her a thousand-fold—
Lies, lies, lies, and sadness.

She is something beyond the words on the page.
She is the perfection that makes me beautiful.
She is the resolution that makes me strong,
The intelligence with which I articulate my declarations,
The energy that animates me,
The voice that rises up and out in a glorious song.
That is the truth worth standing for.
[We all are.]

Future Buddha

My path is about all endless compassion.
My station is at the precipice of incarnation.
My value precedes all label, definition.
My word is nothing short of divine inspiration.
My peace comes from love for what most see as prison.
I forget all distinction between fallen and risen.
I listen and find it in every sound.
I seek nothing and know it's already been found.
My mind is nonlocal, my heart not obscured.
No hurtle is uncrossed. No stone is unturned.

Shapes

Listen, you liar!
Of your hiding and judging,
I have grown tired.

All the world needs you!
The body is right and true.
Step out into view.

I'm sorry to shout.
I buck at your threats, old friend.
I challenge your doubts.

Show them all your shapes,
You dissonant whore and saint.
You are perfection.

Re-Stitch

Messy messy messy
Things are messy and
I'm making new light switches,
Re-stitching leaky bits that escaped me.
In the back and all around,
I'm recalling them now,
Calling them in, let it begin,
A new age of peace and prosperity.
I am a messy changling,
And that's okay with me.
I ride the waves of
Whatever the universe brings to me.
Beautiful center, who are you?
I know you the best.
You're beyond the mess,
A single pointed beauty.
My shoulders melt into the floorboards.
My neck lets it all go,
And my mind is a funny painter,
But there's been a war about the show.

A piece doesn't want the charades,
And the other loves the drama,
A recipe for terror,
Awaiting sudden karma.
I'm sputtering now in my little womb castle—
Nonsensical mystical magic maker MESSY and a riot,
But one piece is a hider.
When the spiders come to get me,
I scream for lust and horror.
All the things I love and hate
Are crisscrossed in strange patterns.
Crisscrossed messages bleed into new order
As I come to center.
A making of a mess
Is now cleaned up in perfect order.
Order order order—what's my order?
What do I want?
A plate of beauty I can munch on,
A tall order of rum,
A pleasure path to cum.
I run away and into
All the things that I love.
Sweet love,
Sticky stuck in the nice relax,
I am a messy changling,
And I like it just like that.

Shadow Fragments
(Hall of Mirrors)

I stand in my hall of mirrors,
Lowly lit with opposing reflections.
Each one is a shadow fragment,
Diverse in their appearances,
Diverse in their aims,
And when the light comes, each disappears.
When the light comes, only I remain.

I see your many faces,
Your millions of eyes,
You—
Swirling and dancing,
Murderous and devouring,
Birthing and creating,
The beacon and the black sky,
Shining your violent vortex,
Emerging out of the backdrop of the blank mind.

I hear the Joker laughing
And saying that I will die.
He sends sudden messages of horror,
Directing the fear inside.
In his trickery, he tells me that I'm the threat,
Hiding sincerity, licking old lacerations.
To show the truth is a risky presentation,
Revealing to a potential threat
One's most vulnerable wound,
And requesting aid but risking
The twisting of a blade,
Or the drinking of blood,
Or a spiteful spitting instead.
So he inflicts the disrespect and hides from solace,
Preparing it all for a comical death.

The lover, my idealist,
So hopeful, so easily enthralled by beauty,
In all sincerity,
Spews succulent words of desire and admiration,
Sensual,
Paints in gradient pastels her picturesque imaginations,
Telling me it is all possible.
The Lover dreams of things and makes them.
She cries in bittersweet rapture
And gasps at each of life's surprises.
Her flowers fall
And make the road
Worth the walk.

The Giant One stores my disregards.
"Forgetting is necessary," he says.
I beckon him to drop it all
And let us pick up the pieces,
Cleaning up the mess together.

The Frail One who wastes away
Becomes more and more brittle each day,
When her will is bypassed and bulldozed.
I see your metaphorical starvation.
I will satiate you.

I've seen Grief itself,
Ashen body
Cusping on crumbling
At any disturbance.
I approached her gloom with such gentleness
In front of her throne of melancholy.
I pressed my forehead to her forehead.
I tended to her collapse,
And on my shoulder, she transformed anew.

I've known the Main.
It discriminates and weighs.
It measures and dictates,
With both hands on the reigns.

I've seen the Beast,
Body foreign and strange,
Carries the world,
An elaborate configuration
Of matter moving through space,
A machine of feeling and action,
Bearing the brunt of pain,
But receiving also the reward of pleasure.

I've seen the one that watches
And reversed into another observer.
And even when I think it's over,
I realize it goes on forever,
In my hall of mirrors.

An Invisible Man

There is an invisible man at the foot of my bed.
He is sitting and watching silently
In a chair
That's not really there.

He wears a military coat in dark navy,
Resembling outer space.
His gaze is imperceptible
Because he has no face,
And there is a vague inclination inside of me
That he wears a hat.

His concealed eyes hold mine steadily,
As I am frozen beneath my sheets
In fear and curiosity.
I banish him away, and he listens eventually,
Flying right out of the window.

Crazy

You make me
Write–your–name–in–blood–on–the–wall
Sacrifice–my–dreams–for–a–ten–minute–call
Mistake–myself–for–a–speck–for–you–to–step–on
Scream–and–wail–for–you–to–call–me–baby
Crazy,
But you couldn't even say you loved me.

Love and Loss

I used to write of heartbreak,
But now I write of love.

To love the truth of change,
To love with palms wide open,
To love from afar when they're gone,
To love even after it's broken.

To know that what you have
Is precious and fragile,
Without any fear of ruin.
To love without begging and clinging,
Without pleading to be snatched from your solitude.

To love by mourning for yourself and them,
To love by braving the truth,
To cry about yourself through their eyes,
To feel their loss of you.

To love freshly but with learned lessons,
And carry the pattern until the very end,
With heart wide open and a smile,
And without the ghosts of the past barging in.

To love to the gallows and to paradise,
To love to heaven and to hell,
But to not forget your own needs,
And to care for yourself as well.

Write!

"**W**rite!"
You say,
With such a view—
The valley and you.
I could never!

Why would I write?
To look down and in
Would be a sin,
With splendor this rare
Enticing my stare.
Why would I write?

Our scene, so gloriously set—
The highest precipice with no net,
Two lovers perched in the clouds.

Then a demand from the muse,
Which (my apologies) I must refuse.
I am far too captivated.

Why would I write
On little blank pages
When here and so near
Are you, my dear,
Bathing in the season's changes?
Why would I write?

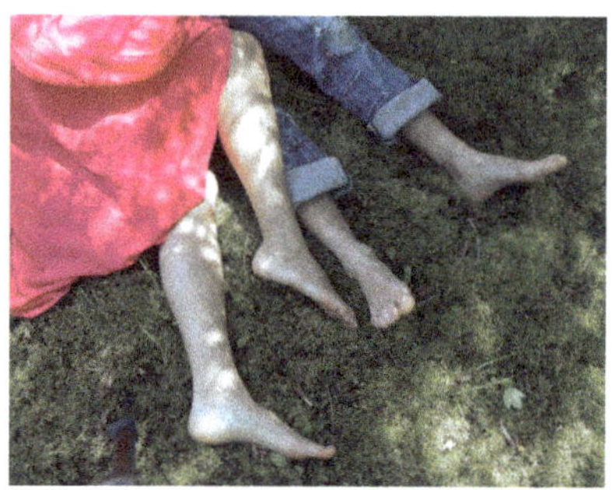

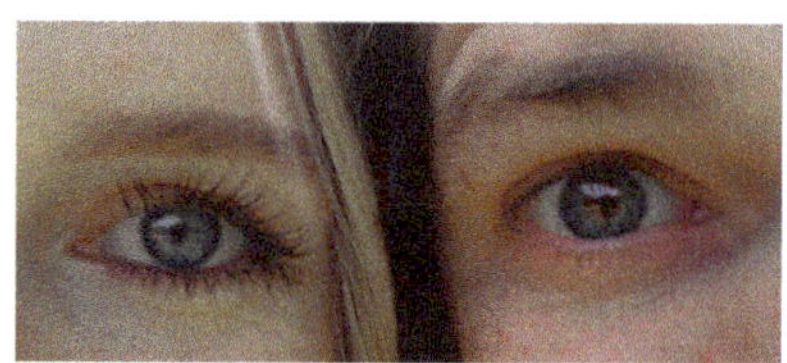

Ode to Roaming Love

Goodbye, Senoia.
I'll always come back to visit.
Identities changed and were lost,
So my search for home persisted.

Middlefield fell through middle earth,
Choices and paths begging to amend.
Two years and change was enough,
Bled dry and bare feet to the dirt again.

This time I'm on the road,
Leaving something mountain–side.
There he stays, and I must go,
But only for a short time.

That something occupies my mind now,
Residing as a permanent fixture,
And if something takes its place for a bit,
It's there in the background as the central picture.

We burned an old Christmas tree on Thanksgiving,
Blazing away our loneliness in holy goodbyes.
While others spit words and ate them,
I promise it's all his, what's mine.

I'll gladly hand over the keys to my car,
When I get back into town.
I'd love to roll the dice on him,
And be done with moving around.

A Cushion for the Soul

A cushion for your soul
If such a thing exists
To narrowly avoid
The existential dread.

A cushion for your soul
Where the floor is unclean,
And the cushion is a vice,
When you need to change the scene.

A cushion for your soul
Is just a short-term solution,
A deal with the devil,
To evade the real resolution.

Forget Your Questions

F orget your questions.
Put them on a shelf,
Or leave them at the foot of your bed,
As you exit the warmth to start your day.
You've already forgotten them anyway.

As you move along, they might bubble up,
But ignore them in earnest.
They are distractions from what is real.
Vacate the strangeness.
Avoid the impulse to feel.

Why solve a riddle
For an answer with little effect?
You are a simple creature,
Looking for simple pleasures,
And nothing more, nothing else,
So forget your questions.
Put them on a shelf.

This War Is a Dance

This war is a dance,
And I deeply adore this endless lore,
The purifying to perfection of every pore,
The gradual entropy into chaos and war,
The truly deranged genius of its performance.

This war is a dance,
A raucous party, and you know it too,
Beyond the word, the scripted truth,
Like a song that makes a crowd jump on cue,
A resonance innate, a deep remembrance.

To their love affair,
We are children,
Tethered,
Like vital life to filthy decay,
Like the right path to the wrong way,
Like the somber night to the shining day,
Intertwined and twinkling.
This war is a dance.

In Search of Plateau

Stop cowering in the face of your fears,
Shrinking away from the things you seek.
Claim it as yours or it never will be.
Keep moving onward, or you will sink,
In this endless game that can never be beat.

Break the bread and drink the broth.
A remedy and poison is there in both.

Say hello, and then bid farewell.
Of whom will stay, you can never tell.

Pray to God; talk in your head.
One day, you'll be forgotten and dead.

Face the demons and let them devour.
To fear and resist gives them more power.

Climb the mountain and search for the peak.
Don't waste a single day of the week.

Storm the barricades. March for peace.
Be the hero in your own destiny.

Roll the dice. Move past go.
Advance forever in search of plateau.

There Will Always Be Doors
That Are Open

Little one of negligence,
By the bottom of the swarm,
Don't shy from the looming vortex.
It's okay to cry for yourself and others,
To be driven from boredom
And compelled out of restriction,
Running to anything that will receive you.
Make note of the welcome,
And don't forget your receipts.
Some things are printed on documents everlasting,
And will be kept in your pocket forever.
To conceive when wanting much,
And concede when receiving little,
It's okay to find the new party no better
And to continue your search,
Injured and shaken, tail tucked under and scurrying away.
You will be received again someplace else.
There will always be doors that are open.

Death Portal

Mysteriously missing meaning clouds the forecast.
You'll look around and find the forgetting of what was asked.
At the edge of what we call known reality,
You find out nothing happens ever.
You forget the fragile focusing.

Too bad if you're tired of being reborn.
It reveals to you the truth,
That what you thought you were is just a filter, broken and worn,
That your loved ones were apparitions of yourself,
That in reality, besides you, there is nothing else.

When the future disappears behind the cloak of invisibility,
No longer held by misguided magicians, hidden figures of history,
At the end of the thing we call time,
A broken bridge becomes a juncture.
Signs and symbols are illuminated,
As are your bad dreams and death portals.

THE ROAD

Two roads diverge...
No, that is a great lie.
In truth, many open before me—
Innumerable.

One is paved with good intentions.
One was deleteriously invented.
One is narrow with shadowed and limited sight.
One is gaping wide and glowing bright.
One is flattened by many travelers' heels.
One is formed of pale dust stirred by wagon wheels.
One is made of leaves, speckled by tree roots and small stones.
One exudes green in sunlight from its overgrowth.
One is paved of asphalt with yellow and white lines.
One is cluttered by historic statues and holy shrines.
One is unmarked through the woods to the left.
One opposes right, leading to the ocean.
One's a trickling stream that quenches small creatures.
One is a tunnel of light with no other features.
One is a rushing river traveled only by boat.
One is nothing more than a tightrope.
One sparkles bright as a hall of mirrors.
One's a darkened corridor lined by furs and materials.
One has a floor lined by spikes and booby traps.
One is untrodden and unchartered by any maps.
One has beings ushering me along.
One is a choir of heavenly song.
One is so quiet, without a soul.
One requires a very large sum toll.
One has walls and floor of blank canvas.
One has swirling color that endlessly dances.

At once, I thought it was two,
But now they are an infinity.
And all of them beckon me right on through.
"I will travel them all," I declare with stubborn certainty.

The Intermission

THE PATH

"I have to go get my shoes, or my feet will bleed!" I yell.

My soles are already raw, tender, and damp from wandering around all this time barefoot. I wince at the concrete, sandpaper slope ahead which beckons me up and onward.

A faceless crowd pushes in the opposite direction, but I'm unsure what they are walking toward. Their attire suggests an outdoor festival set at the turn of the century, equipped with lace parasols and straw boaters. The scene, which oddly feels like I have come alive inside an impressionist painting, feels no more foreign than peering down at my own hands. It is strange, I suppose, but familiar nonetheless.

Looking back to catch a glimpse of whoever I was just yelling to, no person meets my gaze with expectation or concern, and the memory of my prior locale has also escaped me.

Instead of questioning my predicament, I decide instead to move with what was already in motion. I head toward the top of the incline, fervently weaving my way against the grain and navigating the swarm of people between myself and the peak. Little children laugh in cream and pastel outfits, scattering by playfully. Men and women chat casually, their trouser and skirt hems swaying with every shoe stride.

"Shoes... Ah, shoes! That was it," I mutter to myself, partially unaware of the abnormality of my own amnesia.

An inaudible ringing in my head obscures an even more bizarre emptiness, a hazy remembrance that someone was waiting for me, or that I would be right back, but with the details vanished. My body moves like a fish swimming upstream, and the school of bodies thickens as I climb higher, nearly forming an impenetrable current. Their chatter grows indiscernible, and even in the social submersion, I am rather more like an aimless ghost floating through walls in an old house, with the subtlest resistance of matter, but somehow being unencumbered.

I feel strange.

Arriving at the top, I expect to see some logical, expansive continuation of the scene, such as a plateau, but instead, the crowd appears to be manifesting out of thin air, with an abrupt change of scenery standing just beyond.

I peer ahead at the new and sudden puzzle in front of me, which is no expanse nor continuation, but rather something abruptly halted, enclosed, and perplexing. I am now staring into a dark hallway with a metal-teethed rotating door ushering me forward with unexpected seriousness. My mind—once occupied by a low echo, a phantom of vague laughter and conversation—now loudly rings with sudden silence.

What was I doing again? Was I looking for something?

Curious, I move toward the door and slide into the moving aperture, the walls and floors invisible beneath a thick fog. I am flipped around inside the door like a leaf tipping about in a strong gust of wind, then am deposited into a new space just as peculiar as the last. Two doors stand ahead. To the right, an entry filled with color and light gleams toward me. To the left is total darkness.

"A peculiar place," I say to only myself, noticing my solitude.

Giving in to the immediacy of my attention, I look at the door of light and notice how inviting it is. Moving beams of color dance around the space in dynamic chaos. It definitely catches one's attention.

The other entryway is...dark, but I'm oddly curious about it.

Now let's think this through. It is an important decision after all, picking which door to enter. The light path surely seems more pleasant, more welcoming, more obvious. Most people would pick the lighter door, I'm sure of it. The dark path is scary, I suppose, but what if it's a test to see if I'll choose the less obvious option? What if there is some reward for braving the darkness? What if it's a shortcut or if the appearances are intended to mislead me? What if it's a trap?

Analyzing both doorways, I am paralyzed by overwhelming indecision. What is likely only seconds feels like an eternity. Reverse psychologies, reverse-reverse psychologies, doubts, and second, third, and fourth guessings mull about in my mind.

Well, I can't stay here. I have to move forward, and doing so requires a decision.

Suddenly, an impulse of action moves my body before my mind has even fully chosen. I suppose that, emboldened by doubt, the dark path seemed correct somehow. I walk quickly toward the darkness and find myself immersed in a total void that could only be attained in the deepest of caverns—the type of darkness that turns you blind after a period of time.

The same force that prompted the choosing moves me onward. I don't fully comprehend the force, but I press ahead…ahead… ahead…

I'm not sure what I was expecting, but it wasn't this.

No walls, no floor, no end—all vision and direction is obstructed. I turn and feel, turn again and race forward, searching in the darkness to no avail. Spinning in all directions, I realize that the door through which I entered has disappeared. I'm submerged in the dark, alone. I move my hands sporadically, grasping for anything, stumbling a few feet around at a time.

Nothing.

Images of malevolent, malignant, monstrous, malicious faces surface in my imagination, accompanied by terror, a sensation that something is right at my heels, breathing down my back. I run, and run, and keep running, but one realization comes over me: In pure darkness, you can't be sure whether you're running away from or toward something threatening.

At this realization, I stop. Panting and filled with panic, I listen with piercing concentration for a sound of movement. I hold my breath and listen…and listen…and listen…to the sound of nothing.

What have I done? Am I trapped here?

The weight of terror surges throughout my limbs, buzzing in my back and hands. My heart sputters in quick beats, begging for me to flee or fight when there is nothing to run from or fight against. I feel a deepest sense of dread, like the walls are closing in on me, but it's the expansiveness of this space that makes me feel so. I cannot fathom how far it goes, how long this endless void will consume me in this search for something to cling to.

"I made the wrong choice! Let me out! Someone help me! Please! Someone help! Please!"

The sound of my voice carries. There are no echoes here.

Maybe I'm dead. Is this what death is like?

My body shakes in automatic convulsions, a violent trembling overcoming me. My eyes dart around with no object for fixation. My breath is shallow and quick, my thoughts swirling with me trapped beneath. I can't see my own hands or skin, but I am sure that I am stark white with fright and cold to the touch.

Dropping to my knees in exhaustion, the thought of death assuages the panic but invokes something else in its absence: surrender.

I feel like a small child again, tiny in a looming world. The shuttering comes in waves, leading to moments of tension and then moments of release. The surface beneath me has no obvious tactile characteristics. It's as if I'm floating in absolute nothingness. I lay myself down, a future corpse submitting to its fate as food for the darkness.

Acceptance.

The supreme quiet strikes a thought inside, that if it's truly just me in this darkness, there is nothing to be afraid of, no danger to run from, nothing to chase.

Lying here on the ground, I start to hum. My body—still attempting to dispel the nervous energy—is driven to roll over and move. I bend, twist, tap, shake, sway. I follow its impulse, invoking an epiphany, a kind of crazed freedom.

I can do anything I want. No one can hear me. No one can see me. What can I do? What is there to do when no one is around?

I hum to myself. My voice shakes with emotion. My body undulates, my chest rising and falling, my hips swiveling. My whole body moves like a serpent or sound wave. The air around me feels expansive and weightless, and I feel my chest lift with joy.

Liberation.

My voice grows in volume and passion until I am practically yelling the song. A strong sensation wells up in my chest and throat, and laughter escapes. I cackle maniacally and then feel something new. A wailing arises from the deepest part of me, a guttural grief and sadness. I cry so deeply that I dry heave. I am weeping for lifetimes. I am weeping for things I never knew for which I was sorrowful. My grief feels bottomless like this darkness. It's the type of grief that blurs with rage and joy and arousal, then returns back to bittersweet sorrow once again. My expressions eventually wane into stillness, a silence I've never known. The nothingness around me feels like it has seeped inside.

Peace.

Suddenly, a small light emerges in the distance. I can't help but fixate my eyes on that luminosity, which appears to be growing with shocking speed. A tunnel of light engulfs me, and I am rapidly spit out into a small room with two doors.

Turning around, I again see the darkened entryway, and to my left is a door filled with light and color.

What...was that?

Emerging and having been reborn, I see the other entryway, the lighter door, and am urged to explore it also. A third door appears behind me, this time with faint sounds of festivities. I recognize the voices of a chattering crowd and a familiar feeling, like the smell of returning home after a week of travel.

I peer again at the two doors from before, with the presence of a new decision at hand.

Which path will I take?

THE MAZE

Chapter 1 — The Box and the Key

WELCOME TO YOUR DREAMS reads the abrasively graffitied words on the wall ahead. An elegant wooden door looms below, breaking up the visual noise. I almost don't notice the plaque above, which is inscribed with some emboldened text of a five-letter word.

"Limbo," I read out loud, pondering the implications.

What's beyond the door?

Through the black corridor, I step closer, like a newborn with only a singular inclination of crying out—or in this case turning the doorknob. Maybe a non-player character is a better analogy, in which freewill has been stripped in a kind of trancelike flow of slow action, some unseen force moving the story along in perfect timing, or maybe more simply accurate would be a moth to a flame, ignorant desire magnetizing me to its object. In any case, I step up to the door and open it.

"Limbo" is an odd title for such a place. Large and intricate, I am drawn inside with amazement. Color and light, patterns and textures, music, games, furniture, and a variety of objects all lunge toward my retinas and then retreat, enticing me into a game of seek and find. Sounds tinker and flow and click in the background; indistinguishable movement is muffled in a kind of disordered melody.

It so starkly contrasts the dark emptiness of that corridor from which I previously came. No, Limbo isn't a good name. It's more of an intentional chaos, eclectic and enchanting, disheveled and ornate.

I can't help but dart my attention to a small box that has just appeared in my hands, one that feels somehow familiar, but vaguely so. The box, which is roughly the size of a thick book, strikes me as quite attractive, with its pinkish hue and folded and ridged carvings.

A small keyhole and gentle tug at the top clue me in that it has been locked shut, and upon this discovery, I immediately know what my mission is: to find the key!

Briefly scanning the room again, I notice a mirror to my left. Ornate golden hues sparkle around the rim, with a perfect glass surface encased. Dead center is a crystal-clear image of my face. My hair almost matches the golden frame; my eyes and cheeks pick up warmer colors and blues from around the room behind me. I look pretty.

"Like what you see?" asks an unfamiliar voice to my right.

I jolt and immediately notice a young woman standing next to me, maybe in her early twenties. She looks slightly familiar.

"Who are you?" I ask.

"I'm Pawn," she says with a subtle warmth in her demeanor. "I'm glad we both finally made it."

She grabs my hand and takes off with it, my body dragging behind. Each and every object that meets my eyes draws me in closer as I trail behind her, pulling me in opposing directions. Dried flowers and pampas grass fill colored glass vases in purples, ambers, greens, and yellows. Nondescript books—some backward, spines hidden from view—line shelves and sprinkle about the various furniture. Racks of shoes and clothing—furs and leathers, laces and knits, shawls, coats, and dresses—scream at me for further investigation. Vessels, bowls, and baskets in every weave and color hold more bowls and baskets. Taper candles! Spoons! Tapestries! Ornate rugs and beads, lamps, and chairs! Everything with utter allure…even the smell of the place exudes varying layers of enticement and succulence.

"We have to sort these," Pawn says, just after stopping me abruptly atop a flamboyant rug. Kneeling down to some canvas bags, she dumps them into nothing short of a small mountain.

How can so much clothing fit into such small bags?

Instead of pressing the question, I forget my rationality and focus on some of the most beautiful patterns and fabrics I've ever seen.

"Ok…How are we sorting? What's the objective?" I ask while eyeballing one item in particular.

"The objective is to find the things you like. Here, start making piles," she says while gesturing toward a stack of goods. "Separate what you like from what you don't."

One by one, I assess the garments, each item being intently considered for the left or the right pile. My first snag is a wool coat that rests confidently on the bottom of the "like" pile. Inevitably, the stacks become high enough to topple over, motivating me to start second, third, and fourth ones. A sparkling beaded dress…and a bejeweled necklace in jewel tones… and a viridian silk scarf! With each item, a frenzy descends as I am excited more and more in polarized reactions by each piece. A crazed trance comes over me, a trance of indulgence, of frivolity.

"Yes!" I scream with passion. "So beautiful! I'll take them all!"

Pawn looks at me with a blank expression, halting my fervor. Something about seeing her reaction—or lack thereof—reminds me that I was supposed to be doing something.

"Wait a minute, no. I have to go," I say, jumping up abruptly.

Can I really vacate all the beautiful things? Yes, I have to. I need to stick to my mission. Focus. You're looking for a key.

I feel a bit of whiplash at the sudden change, at my abrupt realization. Regrettably vacating the piles of goods with still the same frantic energy as before, I start searching, opening a little tin box and finding nothing, lifting magazines one by one and haphazardly fingering through some of the pages, patting the others to feel for improper objects hidden inside. Drawers of cabinets and corners of rugs are disturbed, all of this hurriedly so as to make up for lost time, like when you remember you had a deadline you were trying to meet but had been sidetracked by making the week's grocery list.

An ornate green and gold table with floral designs and fancy feet (possibly from the Victorian era) catches my attention. On top is a golden pocket watch that is not ticking, and I'm reminded of the written message above the door I last entered: "welcome to your dreams." Turning to check the clocks on the walls, I see that my worry is confirmed. None seem to be working, and all indicate different times.

"Where are we?" I ask, turning to Pawn.

She glares at me with another odd expression, conveying both an understanding and a curiosity, as if she's peering at a lab rat who was unknowingly fed a strange substance and is being closely monitored for reactions. By the look on her face, I'm not sure if she, too, is a lab rat but knows something I do not, or if she herself is the scientist. Either way, she is clearly interested in my sudden change in composure. I feel silly under her steady attention. I've never liked being watched.

Before she can answer, the little wooden box in my hand snags our attention, emanating a low whirring sound, a penetrating humming. As my hands vibrate, Pawn's eyes seize mine, and I'm struck by the look of a creature, otherworldly, who I've never met before.

All music and ambient clatter is drowned out, and my sight grows dark around the periphery, forcing me to fixate all my awareness on her.

"There's something alive in there," she says, gesturing at the box. "Be careful! Look for the door…the door…the door! Look for the door!"

Her voice matches the hypnotic depth of the buzzing somehow, and her words strike fear in me at my root.

"What's happening?" I shout.

No response is given. Luckily, the sound has started to quiet, diminishing until nothing is left but a fainter version of the buzzing in my hands. Pawn's eyes have now returned to her normal demeanor, yet I'm still pressed with the chilling image of her momentary transformation. One of the clothing racks lining the wall has entirely toppled over from the quaking.

What was that?

I tear myself from the thought of the anomaly that just occurred and the pervasive aura left behind. I begin my search again with Pawn trailing behind inquisitively.

"What are you looking for?" she asks.

I pause. The terrifying image of her face and sound of her voice is impressed on my imagination. Goosebumps travel up my spine at the thought of it.

I don't know you. I don't know where I am. Something weird is going on.

"I'm looking for the key to this box," I say reluctantly, presenting her the small object that had mysteriously appeared in my hands upon entering this place.

"How can I help?" she asks.

Ignoring her question, I continue picking up objects, inspecting them, and putting them down. Her steady attention is hard to ignore. I meet her gaze again, briefly, and notice a gentle concern—like that of a dear friend who is holding you as you cry after a hard breakup.

"Why don't we sit down for a moment?" she suggests.

A few feet to the left sits a comfortable-looking sofa I hadn't noticed before. A homey, multicolored plaid pattern generously contrasts my mood, which is starkly bleak. I sit down in a kind of defeat, even in spite of my suspicion of her.

"There… You just rest, and I'll be right here when you're ready to continue your search," she says.

Sitting down in a neighboring chair, Pawn picks up a magazine and opens it, flipping the pages slowly. I feel relaxed suddenly, and the sounds around me blend into an ambient murmur, like a lullaby. A lull descends indeed. Thoughts flow together, one, and another, and I'm not quite grasping anything. Unencumbered, the fleeting moments pass.

Tick…tock…tick...tock…tick…tock…tick…tock…tick……

Like a midday fatigue begging for a nap, I am lost in some hypnotic state, a fogginess, but it doesn't ask for sleep. It's more of a wakeful drifting.

Tick…tock…tick…tock…tick…tock…tick—

"Wait, where is that sound coming from? The clocks don't work," I say, while suddenly sitting up, breaking myself free of the hypnogogia.

I listen, but the clock sound has mysteriously stopped. Pawn once again looks confused and curious.

"I need to keep looking," I say. "I'll be stuck here forever if I don't focus."

Now with feet planted firmly on the ground, I hear a whirring sound down below accompanied by that uncomfortable buzzing. Apparently, Pawn had placed the box at the foot of the couch before my little hiatus.

"It's happening again," I say.

I watch her steadily as the buzzing increases, fearful of whatever spirit or trance might come over her again. My vision narrows and darkens into a tunnel. Her face distorts again. The intensity is greater than before.

"What is this?" I plead.

"Caught in the cycle…You're caught in the cycle. Look for the door…," she says with the strangest expression. Her voice is low and discordant, with a sort of listlessness not previously present.

The moment passes, and the only thing left is a faint buzzing in my feet and legs. The bizarre fit comes and goes quickly, but the disturbance left behind is hard to shake.

"Who are you?" I ask carefully. "Why is this happening?"

She gets up and with an apologetic look, extends her hand to me. The clocks on the walls have fallen, faces shattered and hands bent.

"I told you already. I'm Pawn…the Prodigal," she replies. "That second question is tricky, though. Now, let's go look for that key."

Continuing our search, we end up in an even deeper portion of Limbo. From the ceiling dangles strands of random objects, filling the space entirely from ceiling to knee-height. Some strands hold crystals, labradorite, all sorts of quartz, jaspers, carnelian, and citrine. Others hold gold and silver coins, shells, stained glass and sea glass, translucent helixes, origami creations of birds and stars and geometrical shapes, shoes, hair pins, dolls, nuts walnut hulls, sticks and dried plants, buttons and spools of thread—all suspended randomly in air by various ropes and strings.

"Maybe there's one full of keys," Pawn says, scanning the area.

"It's beautiful," I reply, amazed by the sheer number of objects. "I hope this isn't where the key is, though. We would never find it."

"Hey, look over there," she says, pointing us toward an enclosed area resembling a dining hall.

We walk further to the back left and arrive in a room filled with a banquet table and food and drink. Sparkling dishes with goldtrimmed edges and crystal glasses contain the most impressive variety of edible goods. A fluffy cake with pink powdered coconut dust, a plate of cookies in such an impressive variety that I can't seem to think of a flavor not present, a bubbling tangerine-colored punch, an abnormally large and juicy looking turkey, mysterious and delectable soufflés and casseroles in a variety of dishes, steaming yams and herb roasted potato fingerlings, lobster bisque, mushroom risotto, and more! And more! And more! Every space on the table is occupied by something delicious.

Pawn sits down nearby and gestures at a glorious chocolate muffin with a mound of cream-colored icing—an interesting appetizer choice, but I can't say that I disagree. I take a bite and am engulfed in the most decadent palate of flavors, like someone finally found the exact combination, a profile irresistible and hitting every mark of craving you could've hoped for. Herb-sprigged (with rosemary and thyme) lamb chops catch my eye next—the perfect countering to the sweetness of the cupcake. My mouth waters generously. I pour a glass of purple effervescent liquid, and I make note of big pots of stew, rice, and curry. Something savory and buttery to counteract the sweetness is a great place to start. I should leave adequate room for each item, that way I get to try each dish without stuffing myself.

"I don't know about you, but this is the most satisfying meal I've ever seen," I say, filling a large plate carefully.

After finishing my first helping, I sit back in my chair for a moment of fresh air. However, the box in my lap shifts, almost falling under the table and disrupting my plans for round two of taste-testing. I catch the box and place it squarely in front of me on the table with a sigh of frustration.

"I got distracted again," I say.

"We're just enjoying the amenities," Pawn says with a giggle.

I laugh with her. "It is nice, and the food is fantastic. I really should keep looking for the key, though."

Before I can get out of the chair, the same whirring sound surfaces, and the vibration lights up my whole body. A sour taste forms at the back of my mouth.

Here we go.

This time, the vibration in my limbs is so powerful that it's painful. I look to Pawn and see that twisted expression in her. The tunnel vision has essentially dampened out all other surroundings besides her face, her eyes so penetrating they almost glow. A faint smile turns up the corners of her mouth.

"The key is beyond the door! The door!" she screams.

"Please!" I scream back, my body quaking from the vibration. "What door?"

The episode slowly subsides, and I notice that the chaos has knocked most of the dishes off the table, revealing bits of writing beneath. Holding the box firmly in my left hand, I abruptly swat away the remnants into the floor, revealing some etchings.

Is it a poem?

"It's a riddle!" Pawn exclaims, recollecting herself.

I read it out loud,

"What you seek is one step nearer

Once you find the exit here.

Your passageway is yet to exist,

But will appear should you persist.

Now is time for the table to turn,

But beware, once you exit, you will not return.

The way will appear when the movement is made

To cover me in brick that's already been laid."

Pawn's expression looks a bit excited and disheveled, likely from her prior episode (or maybe she's just that excited by a puzzle).

"Do you get it?" I ask, hoping not to have to think about it.

"Nope. Do you?" she replies giddily.

I'm beginning to think this girl is playing games with me.

"What you seek is one step nearer once you find the exit here. Well, the first few lines are obvious at least," I say.

Pawn says nothing.

"So we're looking for the appearance of a door, and then the key is beyond," I conclude.

"Oh," she says with a hint of confusion. "What if we don't want to leave though."

I stare at her, looking for a sign of dishonesty.

"You really want to stay here? Don't you think something weird is going on?" I ask, waiting for an answer that will indicate whether she is a mad scientist or a lab rat.

"Yeah…but it's so nice. All the food and beautiful things will be left behind. I like it here," she says, subtly pleading.

What's her aim?

"Do you know how we got here, or what's going on? Because I don't. I'm supposed to find the key and see what's in this box," I say.

I notice her expression, which is teetering on sadness and overwhelm. I'm still not sure if she is a fellow rat or a scientist, but I feel bad for her for some reason.

"Look, you can decide later if you want to leave or not, but at least help me find the door so that we can have the option."

"Yeah…Okay," she replies.

"So…we're supposed to cover the table in bricks. Seems odd. Have you seen any bricks in this place?" I ask.

"Doesn't it say we need to cover the table in bricks that were already laid, as in, they were already built into something?" she asks flatly.

"How are we going to cover a table with something that's already been built?" I ask, surprised by her conclusion.

"Beats me," she says.

I sigh and read it one more time.

"Now is time for the table to turn…So we turn the table. What about a brick wall? We could press it against a wall," I say.

Inspecting one of the floral wallpapers in the dining room, I feel around for indentations where the mortar joints would be.

"Hand me one of those steak knives."

I make a gash in the wallpaper, peeling away a small piece of Limbo and revealing red brick beneath.

"Too easy," I say. "Here, help me move this."

We push aside a console table blocking the nearest wall and take down a hanging painting. Pawn looks puzzled at the artwork, which depicts a garden scene with a cute little cottage.

"That's nice," I say to her curiously.

"Yeah," she says with an odd, sad expression.

"Do you...not like it?" I ask.

"No, it's not that. It just reminds me of something."

I ignore the comment. We hoist the table up onto its narrow side, so that two legs are up in the air, and two are sticking out near the floor. We then scoot it against the wall, pressing the tabletop flush to the wall. A kind of clicking occurs, and that same buzzing begins, only this time, Pawn doesn't become entranced. The table seemingly fuses to the wall, growing a round, golden doorknob and wooden trim.

"I can't believe that actually worked!" I say. "Are you coming?"

With a reluctant nod from Pawn, I open the door, and peer in.

No. This is all wrong.

The darkened corridor that I came from stretches out in front of us, and the door through which I entered laughs at me from across the hall.

It's a circle? Can I not escape?

"I've already been here," I say.

I walk closer and notice that the surrounding walls are blank.

"Wait...There's no graffiti."

"Huh?" Pawn mumbles.

I walk briskly through the dark up to the new door and notice that the plaque above, instead of reading "Limbo," says "Jupiter."

"That's a relief. I thought for a second that we're stuck here forever," I say.

"Would it really be so bad?" she replies.

I turn to her and smile, noticing that Limbo's door has vanished behind her, leaving just the plaque and those graffitied words: "welcome to your dreams."

"Fingers crossed there's a flashing sign pointing to a key," I say sarcastically before opening Jupiter's door.

The space is barren, a wasteland of flat expanse with no greenery, no objects in sight besides some dead trees. The wind blows heavily, and there is a hint of mist and snow in the air. Out in the distance, a mountain—or maybe a pyramid—rises on the skyline, with a piercing light at the top. I can't tell if the light is originating from inside the peak or is shining onto it.

"Freezing," Pawn says, "We should've brought some clothes from Limbo."

"There's no way we'd survive out there. Am I supposed to go to the light?" I ask, feeling overwhelm sink in once again.

Something tells me not to go inside, so I pull us back into the corridor and sit down on the ground. Jupiter's door disappears, leaving us with only a small, circular window overhead, and a half-moon shines through, acting as a spotlight to the otherwise dark hallway.

"Well, I guess that decides that," I say, glad that I don't have to walk through Jupiter's wasteland. "I don't understand. You kept saying look for the door, and we found the door. Where is the key?"

I can see the faint outline of Pawn's face.

"Maybe there's another door," she says.

Another door?

Confusion, frustration, and defeat boil up inside of me.

"I think I'm being tricked."

Pawn tilts her head like a dog trying to understand human words.

"Who would be tricking you?" she asks.

Her illuminated face glows in the moonlight, framing her as either a bonfire-storyteller of a tale of horror or a romantic lover during a late-night rendezvous. I stay silent.

"It's just us and the moon now," she says. "We should have stayed in Limbo."

"I'm supposed to find the key," I say lowly.

The moon's light shines in as a singular beam. At the base of the ray, something catches my eye—a small square seam in the flooring. I feel the ground, analyzing the square.

"I think it's a door," I say after noticing a small finger hole.

I stick my finger in and pull around until the piece of flooring swings open, hinging on one joint.

"Does that count as a door?" Pawn asks sarcastically.

Feeling around the bottom, my fingers bump into something.

"It's here," I say, trying to mask my excitement.

With the key, which is cool to the touch and looking like an antique from the nineteenth century, and the box in hand, I ask, "Are you ready?"

She nods in the moonlight.

"Okay, here we go."

As I turn the key and open the lid, a whirring sound emanates so loudly that it's as if we're standing next to an airplane. The buzzing reverberates the whole corridor, like the sound of a high-speed bullet train. I feel a warping sensation, an extreme case of vertigo, followed by being lifted off of my feet.

Everything goes dark.

In the hall sits a small box, with door ajar and not a soul in sight.

Chapter 2 – The Bow and the Arrow

Dizzy…I am so dizzy.

I haven't fully landed here just yet. Having opened my eyes only seconds ago, I see that I'm outside, surrounded by glowing green as the sun shines through the leaves.

Where am I?

On the ground around me are winding brick paths, leading to a focal point—me (or rather, where I'm standing). The surrounding area appears to be a walking labyrinth, with the ends trailing off as serpentine paths throughout the garden.

A man walks confidently toward me, as if an old friend were greeting me after being away for a year. He's smiling and reaching toward me with a playfulness.

"Hey, you," he says. "I'm glad we both made it."

"Who are you?" I ask.

He stares at me with a smirk, shifting his weight, seemingly waiting for me to catch up.

"Pawn?" I ask, now remembering that same greeting from before and recognizing something in his expression.

"The Protector," he says with a nod and a semi-flirtatious sparkle in his eyes.

"Why are you…a guy now?"

He ignores my question and grabs my hand, just like before, pulling me deeper into the garden and following one of the brick paths.

"Where are you taking me this time?" I ask, noticing how attractive he…or…she is. The way he smiles at me makes my stomach and chest flutter, and now, as I'm trailing behind, I'm noticing the warmth of his hands and prominent veins in his arms.

"Like what you see?" he asks, with just one side of his mouth upturned. "I know it's probably a shock to you."

He probably felt that I was staring at him—checking him out. I look in the opposite direction without a response.

We arrive at the outskirts of a small meadow, surrounded by willows and hemlock trees. Our path took us right to this clearing, and I feel as though I've stepped into an old painting. Everything is soft and light. Branches of pink flowers droop to knee level, forming a canopy and curtain all around. We stop at the base of one tree.

"So beautiful," I mutter.

"Should we keep walking? Or should we…?" he asks, moving a little too close for comfort. He grabs the sides of my face and kisses me, pressing firmly into my body and inserting his tongue into my mouth.

"Hey! What the hell are you doing?" I exclaim.

"Don't worry. In this version, we're together," he replies. "Isn't it nice?"

He again moves toward me, and I see him as I saw Pawn…the first Pawn…for the first time. The same eyes shine through, no matter the transformation. I feel an electric, warm sensation in my crotch. Am I turned on?

"I don't know what you mean by version, but I'm a little startled," I say, pushing him back and looking down at my feet.

"That's okay," he says, "Take your time."

My attention is brought to a little cottage to the right, which I somehow didn't notice before.

"Is that your home?" I ask.

"It's our home," he says back.

With a little hop to the side, Pawn stretches out an open palm and nods toward the house. I take his hand, and we walk down the path toward the front door, my attention steadily on the feeling of his hand in mine. His skin is so smooth. I'm struck by the feeling of familiarity, like muscle memory taking over after having forgotten how to play a song on the guitar. This feels like the right tune.

I look back in the direction of the labyrinth, which is now out of sight, and as we reach the part of the path next to the cottage, my attention is diverted to a sudden feeling of something crawling up my leg. I look down and see hundreds of insects, spiders, centipedes, millipedes, and beetles, making their way up my legs and body. I scream, startling Pawn, who turns around in shock.

Before we can do anything, a large snake slithers out from beneath the porch, coiling briefly and looking in our direction. It is the largest snake I've ever seen, with a head the size of a cantaloupe.

Its body is the strangest color of deep green, and its eyes glow in pomegranate pink, nothing less than a proper monster. I slowly back away.

The snake advances toward me and turns upright, standing up on the back of its tail, its head level with my head, and moving toward me at an increasing rate. I back away quicker and quicker, feeling more and more terrified. I've entirely lost sight of Pawn and feel completely alone to defend myself. The snake levitates toward me, ready to strike.

"Some protector you are," I mutter to myself.

Avoiding the first strike, I grab its neck and move my hands toward its head, maintaining a firm grip and preventing it from striking me.

It's too strong for me, and I sense that I will lose grip quickly. The snake snarls and hisses, bearing its fangs and vowing to sink them into me. I cry out for help, exhausted from wrestling the monster. Finally, Pawn comes running out of the front door with a bow and arrow. The snake's head is starting to slip as Pawn confidently aims and releases, sending an arrow straight into the snake's head, which deeply disturbs me. I can see Pawn beyond, and his expression is disconcerting. I realize why when I feel the blood running down my face.

The arrow, which shot entirely through the snake's skull, had apparently pierced my forehead. A strange buzzing radiates throughout my head, and it…feels good. Covered in refuse, I drop the snake's body into a small pond to my left and then collapse.

I wake up to a little pressure in my forehead and sit up to find myself indoors. The room is quaint and clean, and, strangely, the couch that I'm on is the same couch I laid on before in Limbo. Pawn sits in that same matching plaid chair with a book. What a bizarre instance of déjà vu.

"Are you feeling okay, love?" he asks gently.

"I'm okay. Where are we?"

"We're in our living room," he says, grabbing my hand. "Would you like a tour?"

I don't think I want a tour. I'm beginning to tire of this amnesiac sensation. Everything is so familiar, yet so alien.

"No," I say.

"I'm sorry I didn't get to you sooner," he says with a regretful expression. "You were very brave."

I look down at my hands to avoid his sincere, concerned expression.

"You'll at least want to look in there," he says, gesturing toward an entryway to a conservatory of sorts.

"Why? What's in there?" I ask.

He hesitates. "You'll just have to see for yourself."

I open the frosted glass door and almost collapse at the sight of what's inside. A room made entirely of glass—from ceiling to walls—houses not only an impressive spread of plants but also a giant tank filled with something so terrifying and beautiful, so bewildering to consider. The creature floating within inspires an intense surge of emotion. Wonder and awe, mania, hysteria, frenzy, fear, shock, and dread—I feel it all. A dragon…in a fish tank. Her scales shimmer iridescently. Her wings hug her body. Her eyes plead with me. A plaque above reads "Venus."

I walk over to meet her gaze, which feels like the right thing to do.

Old friend, here you are. Who has put you in a cage?

She undulates slowly in the water, her body moving like a wave. I am trembling next to her, like a tiny rabbit at the feet of a ferocious tiger.

"There's something in you. Don't be afraid," she says. (Or did I imagine it?)

A sudden impulse comes over me to break her free, to grab something hard or sharp and extricate her from her glass prison. I raise my hand to touch the glass, but Pawn touches my shoulder softly, stopping me from making contact.

"Not yet," he says. "Follow me. I want to show you something."

I walk behind him into a dimly lit room off of the living room—an office or parlor—with books lining shelves going up as high as three stories. A ladder with wheels beckons me to inspect the bookshelves from top to bottom.

"Here. Sit," he says, gesturing at the desk, "and close your eyes."

I shyly pop up onto the desk and cover my eyes with my hands, my legs dangling below. I wonder if he's going to make another move on me. The bandage on my head is starting to annoy me. I rub the spot behind the tape and cotton gauze where I was penetrated by the arrow.

"Open," he says, tapping my knee.

I open my eyes and see a gold key dangling at the end of a chain.

"The key!" I exclaim.

He nods.

"So she really was you the whole time—I mean—the other Pawn," I say.

He steps back a bit, lowering the key. "I'm a lot of things. It's not one or the other," he says, noticing my annoyance at the bandage.

"The important thing for you to know is that I'll always be here for you when you need me."

His expression looks sad as he removes the bandage from my head.

"What's wrong?" I ask.

"It's just that I wish we could stay here indefinitely," he replies.

"You don't like leaving, huh?" I say playfully. "The other Pawn wanted to stay in Limbo, too."

He looks up with a serious look and puts the key and chain over my head, hanging it against my chest. I notice the position of his body and mine and feel a magnetizing pull toward him, especially at the hips. The warmth and electricity are back, softly radiating up into my stomach and heart. He feels even more familiar now, like someone I've known and missed for a very long time and am just finding again. I grab his shirt and pull him in closer.

"Are you feeling less startled now? Are you still confused?" he asks, his voice low and slow, almost at a whisper.

I move my hips to the very edge of the desk and press myself into him.

"Actually, I'm feeling quite lucid," I say.

Some sort of physical memory takes over. I feel the anticipation and the sadness and the passion with him. Even though my mind cannot recall whatever history we have, my body remembers it well, and I know that I am bound to him somehow. I can feel his sadness for my absence. I am happy to be with him now. The subtle remembrance of a great love lost and then found again pours out of me in arousal and excitement and grief. I forget all else, the key and Limbo, the snake. I forget what I'm searching for. I forget that I am searching.

We make love, and I weep.

"You know what you have to do," he says at the closing, bluntly changing demeanor to that of a fellow soldier ready to risk it all. "Make sure that after you do it, you get to the center of the labyrinth. I'll wait there for you."

"Do it? Do what?" I say with confusion.

He continues dressing and avoids even making eye contact.

The dragon. Right.

"What will happen if I release her?"

He continues his avoidance.

"How should I break it?" I ask.

A hint of flirtation returns to his eyes. "You don't need anything but this," he says, placing my index finger in his mouth.

I recall a moment from Limbo in which his previous version licked cupcake icing off of her fingers. The strictly platonic feelings I had for the first Pawn leave me wincing at this one's amorous gestures.

In the conservatory, the beast has become more active, waving her body quicker and making rapid twitching movements.

Can she anticipate what is to come? Does she feel how I feel? I slowly move toward her. Why am I doing this again? Why was she caged to begin with?

The doubts and questions are drowned out by some deeper intuition. Her aggravation has increased, her body undulating quicker and with sudden twitches.

"I will free you. Don't worry."

My trembling hand reaches up to the glass, and with one finger, I tap it. Suddenly, like a shimmering bubble, the surface pops into nothingness, temporarily suspending the water in open air—the calm before the storm. I am suddenly face-to-face with the dragon, with no barrier separating us, when the great flood erupts.

I have already started retreating when the water consumes me, engulfing me in the rushing current. The pressure rises in turbulent swirls, and I tumble inside. It didn't occur to me that the water would have such force. Now floating high above and looking down at the checkered floor nearly thirty feet below, I realize that the tank of water has filled the entire conservatory from floor to ceiling.

Will I drown? How long will I be able to hold my breath? Where is the beast? My panic is sliced through by the enormous serpentine eyes that meet mine merely feet away.

"Hold onto me," she says silently.

I grab on to one of the horn-like spikes across her spine, which suddenly propels me through the water. She picks up speed, doing a loop, until I'm almost unable to keep a grip. I've lost my bearings and am running out of oxygen.

"I'm going to drown! I need air!" I try to tell her so via some telepathic conveyance.

She now is headed straight for the ceiling and shatters it violently, shielding me from the shards with her wings. Something about the explosion triggers what seems like a memory.

I am peering out of a window in the conservatory, and Pawn comes up behind me, moving my hair from my neck, then kissing it softly.

"Did you forget something?" he asks playfully, handing me a mug of something warm.

"I wish we could stay here indefinitely," I recall him saying only minutes ago.

Now in open air, I gasp for oxygen. A giant gust of fire erupts from the dragon, and she swoops down close to the meadow. The same wings that shielded me from the glass now knock me from her back.

I shield myself from the impact and roll into the grass, still gasping.

"Hurry!" I hear Pawn screaming through the trees, and I start to stumble in his direction. He's yelling something else indiscernible.

I look back at the beast, who is now descending from her initial blast off. A giant ball of fire booms out of her fanged mouth, hitting the willows closest to the cottage, then the cottage itself on a front corner.

"No!" I exclaim, moving toward her in hopes of shielding the meadows and home from her wrath.

"Come on!" Pawn screams. "Get to the center!"

I turn around and pick up speed as another gust of hot air warms my back. The dragon has been locked up for a long time. She is angry and will burn it all. I bet she wouldn't listen to me, and I'd die trying to save this place. I run along the brick path as fast as I can possibly go, returning to where it all started. When I round the corner, I see Pawn in the middle of the labyrinth.

"Hurry! Follow the path!" he says with a circular motion of his hands.

He wants me to actually navigate the walking labyrinth, instead of darting straight for him. I can hear the dragon spitting fire in the distance.

"Why did we release her?" I yell with tears welling up in my eyes.

After meeting a few dead ends, I finally get to him. One big embrace from him brings me so much comfort.

"I remembered something! You brought me tea," I say.

He smiles. "You forgot something," he says, holding up the chain and key. I realize I must have taken it off during our encounter in the office.

"Thank you," I say as he places it back around my neck. A small stone pyramid rests in the central point, just behind Pawn.

"Once we touch that, we won't be coming back here…for a while," he says.

I feel his sadness. "The house—it's going to be destroyed…and all the gardens," I say.

"It's okay. It will regrow and rebuild, even better actually."

"And will I see you again…in this form I mean?"

"Yes, someday."

I kiss him and turn to the stone, knowing that the beast will be coming for us soon.

"On three?" he asks.

"On three."

Chapter 3 – The Compass and the Door

I open my eyes to fire. A night sky sparkles with unusual commotion as a constellation of a hunter falls from outer space, breaching the atmosphere. All around me rain arrows and darts of blazing debris. I start to run for cover, but as soon as I move my legs, they press against a bundle of ropes and fabrics, which wrap me up safely and suspend me in mid-air. Where they attach to, I cannot say, but instead of running, I am swinging through space.

The hunter constellation resembles a giant painted statue, a memorial of some god falling from heaven to Earth, wreaking an otherworldly chaos. As if frozen in his descent, the constellation sits partly inside the atmosphere and partly out, hugging his bow to his chest as he falls earthside into the terrestrial domain. The red planet—Mars—dangles in the sky just beyond.

I move my body and recollect how to stop and go, move sideways, move backways, and flip. Loops and knots hold me in a series of undoing and reforming. Weightless, I am dodging the space debris in a graceful dance. The degree of control over my movements, the power and visceral exertion intoxicate me with excitement as the wind blows around me, even through the smoke and mayhem.

In the wide expanse of sand and rock below, I see a small rectangular structure. I lower myself in the materials, unwrapping and sliding down, until I am close enough to see what is there.

It's a...cage?

Something is in there. I leave my flowing fabrics and plant my feet on the ground, approaching the cage with caution. There, sitting with legs crossed in some bizarre calmness, a monkey sits undisturbed by the apocalyptic nature of the surrounding scene. It pays no mind to me as I walk closer to its cage.

"Aren't you afraid?" I ask, looking up to the sky and hearing the sounds of cataclysm (which are surprisingly quiet).

The stars glimmer past the chaos, and the peaceful sky is fixed above. This moment of stillness feels inappropriate given the dangers at hand. Something about the monkey's demeanor strikes me as human. He's likely around four feet tall—the height of a human child, but he could probably do some damage if he attacked me, though.

I lift up the latch on the cage hesitantly, and he looks up at me with a kind of neutral, vacant expression. Upon opening the door, a sudden transformation in his expression takes over—a smile.

"You came! Took you long enough," he says.

The little monkey walks over and grabs my hand. His voice sounds like a young boy, maybe eleven or so.

"You were expecting me?" I ask.

With a little twinkle in his eye, he says, "Of course. I'm always here for you when you need me."

No, it can't be.

He returns my blank stare with an expectant smile.

"I'm Pawn… Pawn the Pilgrim (this time anyway)," he says, with an uncanny tone in his voice.

I remember Pawn—the other Pawn—and our time together in the garden and how deeply I felt for him. This little monkey surely can't be the same man I had met before. I somehow feel responsible for him now.

"Haven't you figured it out yet? We're in this together," he says with the innocence of a childhood friend that is about to fight imaginary monsters with you in a fortress made of bed sheets and pillows. "We should take cover, though," he adds, pointing toward a cave entrance at the perimeter of the wasteland.

What appeared to be a desolate cavern from a distance is actually a kind of passageway, with many people stationed at its entrance. People sit in clusters, talking and eating, peering out at the commotion, and walking from the cave's mouth further toward the back. A makeshift stone table houses a meager pot of stew with a line forming against the wall.

"Hey, what's happening? Is there somewhere safer to take cover?" I ask one of the cave people before noticing a faceless head looking back in my direction.

"You can't talk to the faceless here," Pawn says. "Don't worry. We can pass through a tunnel in the back."

Remembering the dark corridor and feeling an uneasiness in my gut, I say, "I think I'm done with dark tunnels."

"Don't worry. It's just a short passage," he says. "Here, you'll be needing this."

The little monkey hands me a small circle with an arrow inside, which points directly toward the tunnel. I turn it in circular directions, discovering that it's a compass but with no etchings for the four directions. I hold it close to my chest and then place it safely in my pocket. As we walk toward the darkness, something about its presence comforts me as we press ahead, especially in light of my overwhelming desire to turn back and evade this place.

The tunnel dumps us into a smaller room with two doorways, one spilling out light, color, and sound, and the other pitch black.

Not the dark again.

"Which way does the arrow point?" Pawn asks, standing on the front pads of his feet.

I take the compass out of my pocket, and luckily, it's pointing toward the lighter door.

"We go right," I say.

Without a second thought, we stride toward the door and enter the light. Music plays loudly from all around, without a local source. I can't make out any particular instrument or lyric. It's as if all instruments are being played at once, forming a celestial yet terrifying surround-sound. Melodies drastically shift. To follow one chain of sound is pointless, as each suddenly folds into something else. A kaleidoscope of colors dance in elaborate shapes along the sky, morphing continuously into new…new…new…always a new shape. Nothing here is static or stagnant. Nothing here is calm, or boring, or bland, or low. Shapes dance along the ceiling and walls, as if it's all alive and pulsating, swaying, breathing. In the air are little floating things resembling bubbles, but also petals or little balls of cotton. *POP!* A small mark is left behind on my hand from where one landed and erupted in a tiny explosion. Beams of light stream all around, like being inside one of the sun's rays. My eyes hurt from the sheer amount of visual stimulus and saturation.

To my side is little Pawn, who is slowly walking alongside. On his face is an expression of pure awe. He is holding my hand gently, and I hadn't even noticed.

"So beautiful," he says.

Looking down, I notice that my hands look really far away. Time moves in short bursts of super-speed, then in slow motion. My feet leave phosphorescent imprints along the ground, and growing in their place is some strange mossy material, leaving damp, fuzzy footprints behind. Traces of light stream behind my feet and behind my every movement. The feeling I have here is indescribable. It feels as if I'm not meant to be here as a human, as if this isn't meant for human eyes. I begin to cry and feel a swell of emotions rising, like a flower blooming inside a tiny glass box, with little room to blossom. I can't fully describe the feelings, but they teeter between horror and ecstasy.

"Beautiful," I echo.

We continue walking straight ahead through the light. I know that if I stay here, I won't be able to leave, that I will break down. Up ahead, a doorway appears, and we exit into somewhere new, where the only thing jarring my perceptions is the ringing silence.

What was that?

Three more doors stand before us—this time all shut. The one to the left is small, I'd say about three feet high and three feet wide—a perfect square—painted in a bright yellow with a little brown knob. The paint looks worn and chipped, as if it leads to an attic in someone's well-loved home.

The door to the right, however, is tall and rounded at the top and is large enough to fit a giant. With a stunning blue color and delicate motifs, it strikes me as an entryway to an ancient palace's great hall—or something like that.

The door in the center is just a regular old door, painted green and with a pretty golden handle.

"I'm getting really sick of doors," I add.

Pawn looks up at me with that knowing look, like he did when he was in the other two forms. I see it now—the resemblance. I get why he wanted to stay in the garden.

"Check the arrow," he says.

"I hope it's pointing straight toward the blue door," I say.

I reach into my pocket and don't feel the compass, invoking that unsettled feeling in my gut once again.

"It's gone," I say, slightly panicked and patting down my body for other resting places.

"You can follow me," a small voice says from behind.

I jump and turn around with Pawn clinging to my hips. A cat is sitting a couple feet away, staring at us intently.

"Hello?" I ask fearfully.

"You can follow me," she repeats, strutting around us with a confidence only felines possess.

She is black, which is probably why we didn't see her initially. A white spot on her back is in the clear shape of an arrow pointing in the direction of her line of sight. Pawn looks at me again, this time with his usual childlike demeanor. He shrugs and walks behind her as she leads right up to the green door in the center.

"Do you still have the key?" Pawn asks. "These doors are locked."

I reach up and pat my chest, feeling for a chain.

"I do."

Looking to the other doors, I notice that all three have little keyholes on them, in the same size and shape. I look down at the little cat once more who is pawing the bottom of the green paint. I unlock the door and turn the knob.

Does this key really open any door?

Following the compass, we arrive on the top of a grassy hill, surrounded by nothing more than the spotless blue sky and the endless continuation of green pasturelands.

"Which way now?" I ask the cat.

She sits onto her back legs and looks up, with her front two paws dangling against her belly.

"Up? But how?"

She looks at me and Pawn. Her eyes look like jade stones—green like the door, green like these hills, with a thin vein of darkness in the center.

"Make a sacrifice," she says.

"How would we do that?" I ask.

Pawn has plopped onto the grass and is enjoying the scenery, staring up at the sky.

"I like it here. Can we stay for a while?" he asks.

"We need to follow the arrow, don't we?"

I turn to the cat, who has one front paw on the earth and the other raised, still with her face turned skyward.

"What are we supposed to sacrifice?" I ask again.

The cat plants both paws and looks at me with a piercing assuredness. "Place anything you are willing to leave behind at your feet," she says.

"Anything?"

The cat has returned to her pointing, and I pick her up kindly.

I suppose I will take that literally. If it's anything, that's easy.

Tearing off a strand of my hair, I ready myself for placing it on the ground, which could spur some strange event. Anything can happen after all.

The cat squirms in my hand a bit. "You both will have to make a sacrifice to exit," she says.

"Okay, pluck one of yours," I say to Pawn. "You have plenty to spare anyway."

The little monkey boy sighs and stands, as if his mother just told him he has to go clean his room. To see such an expression in a creature of his kind is somehow adorable yet unnerving. He plucks a hair from the crown of his head.

"Ready?" I ask. "On the count of three, we're going to place the hair at our feet."

"One."

I hold the cat snuggly under my arm.

"Two. Three."

Just as the strands of hair meet the grass, two trees spring up from the soil and grow at an incredible rate, with us clinging on as best we can. The trees grow up tall…up… and up… and up… we go. A black hole in the sky swallows us, and I can see below the green disappearing, eclipsed by the closing of the portal.

Our new room isn't far off from the last. This time, four doorways lie ahead. Frustration immediately boils to my surface.

"I can't take this anymore! When will this end? Where are we even trying to go?" I explode.

I set down the little black cat, and she sits at my feet, looking ahead to the doors.

Pawn backs away from me, looking at me with an inquisitiveness not unlike the first Pawn, when I frantically was searching for the key. I again feel odd under such acute attention.

"How can I help?" he asks.

"How should I know? I have no idea what's going on."

The cat is now over at the doorways assessing the situation. I join her, and from what I can tell, we are in quite a predicament. The far-left door is a narrow corridor with burning red sand and stone. Passing through seems impossible. Next to that is a dark entry, which I can't see far into. Lifeless, gnarled trees and thorny brush obscure the view. The third door is probably the most eerie of them all—gray walls with a pool of water below. The water is as black as the night sky, with no telling what lurks beneath the surface. A continuous motion of gentle waves ruffles the otherwise still liquid. To the far right is a doorway with even worse visibility. The thickest of fogs clouds the room. The cat still paces from doorway to doorway, inspecting each thoroughly.

"Hey, there are words above," Pawn says, excited with his discovery.

Just above each frame are etched words, faint enough to go unnoticed unless one really paid attention.

"Disaster, Distress, Disease, Disorder," I read.

"Disaster," the cat says, pointing to the far left.

"Wait a minute. That doesn't seem like our best option," I say in protest.

"Disaster is the way," she replies.

I go over and inspect the far-left door once more. The sand and jagged stone glow in ember-oranges and reds, covering the entire corridor from wall to wall. Steam emits from the ground, and no areas appear to be cool or safe to walk on.

"We can't go that way. Why would you pick that one? We will burn up in there," I say to the cat.

"You're equipped," she says, pointing toward my feet.

I look down and notice a pair of hefty black boots on my feet, which feel particularly heavy.

Were those there before?

I walk over to the "Distress" doorway and strain to see any clear paths between the jagged branches and briars. I might have chosen this door, but it is quite thick. We would likely get marled inside by the thorns. I walk next door to "Disease." There's no way around the pool of water. The only way past is through, and this one would probably be my last pick. Even aside from the disturbing name, I don't love being in eerie waters with no visibility beneath. The far-right door, "Disorder," is a contender for first pick.

"I'm not sure I can pass," Pawn says. "I'm not wearing any shoes."

"Are you sure about this? The 'Disorder' door has the least obvious danger. It could just be heavy fog all the way. Why pick one that we know is catastrophic?"

"Disaster is the way," the cat repeats.

I look down to my boots again and notice the sturdy soles. Maybe they are heat and flame resistant.

"Okay, in that case, we only have one potion. I'm going to have to carry you both, aren't I?"

The little monkey boy and black cat stare at me with what would be raised eyebrows (if they had them).

"If we're going to follow the arrow, let's get it over with. Pawn, climb on my back," I say.

Holding the black cat in one arm and with Pawn clinging to my back, we head into the door of embers with me carefully navigating. I start out by only stepping on sand, avoiding any stones for fear of making a wrong move and toppling us all over. The sand, however, proves to be deep enough that it shifts easily beneath my boots, flinging up burning grains onto my legs. In some spaces, the sand isn't visible enough between the rocks, so I hoist us onto the flattest stones I see and try my best to keep my balance with all the added weight.

"The boots won't last," the cat says, and I look down briefly to see burn marks along the bottoms. I pick up the pace.

"Okay, make sure you don't move. It could throw off my balance," I say.

In the distance, the exit appears, and in the heat of the moment, I become furious at the sight of it.

"What the hell am I doing?" I scream. "The doors never end!"

"Keep going! It'll be worth it. I promise," Pawn says, with a hint of fear in his voice, possibly wondering if I'm going to drop him there and make a run for it.

My legs are stinging from the heat, and I'm losing my grip strength. I'm not sure how much life is left in my boots, and I can't look down to check. If I trip or lose balance, we will all go down and be severely burned. One last little burst of energy surges through me as I reach around twenty feet from the exit. I can feel the heat on the balls of my feet. The boots must be wearing down quickly.

"Go, go, go!" Pawn yells.

"Aaaaahhhhhhhhhhhhhh!" I scream.

I flop over into the doorway, sending Pawn and the cat rolling onto the floor. I crawl away from the heat and hurriedly untie the boots, peeling them off mostly undamaged feet. A minor burn on the side of my left foot pulsates.

"We made it!" Pawn celebrates, giving me a big hug.

Ahead are hallways going in many different directions, only they are short, as if you have to crawl through them on your hands and knees. Still panting, I roll over onto my back and stare at the ceiling blankly, contemplating the endlessness of it all.

"Are we still stuck in Limbo?" I ask Pawn.

He doesn't respond.

"When will we arrive? We just keep going and going. When will we get there? When will we be done?"

A short silence reminds me that I still don't really know Pawn, or whether he...or she...is a lab rat or a scientist.

"I'm not sure how to answer that. Let's keep following the arrow, okay? Everything will be okay," he says, tugging at my arm.

"I wish I was back in the garden with the other you."

I flip over and move to my hands and knees.

"Lead the way," I say to the cat.

We follow her through one hallway with me crawling and Pawn hunched over. Luckily for the cat compass, she has no problem with navigating this place. With one turn around a corner, I see cats all throughout the hallway, but they are unusual. Each of them has unique coloring and patterning. One cat is a deep iridescent blue with hints of purple. Another one walks by, rubbing its tail on my leg. It has detailed black and white symbols all over, almost like some ancient or futuristic written language. A bright pinkish red cat sits over by the wall, licking its front paw. Others are coming and going from little cubbies inside the walls.

I crawl over to one cubby and notice that everything inside is shrunken down to fit the space, as if a room full of objects made for my proportion had been miniaturized into toy models. One gray cat with long fur sits in a recliner, and another has hopped up onto a little mahogany coffee table, tipping over a miniature bowl of popcorn. In spite of the confined feeling from the narrow hall, the place is quite cute.

To the right is a pink and lime green room with transparent acrylic furniture. The compass cat guides us by, meowing at a brown and cream striped friend. We make a turn around another corner and pass a cubby with a miniature clothing rack full of color, bold patterns, and dramatic textures. Little hats hang on tiny hooks on the walls, and small shoes and boots line the floor beneath. Pawn looks at me with an amused expression.

The next hall has a cubby containing a soccer court. We keep crawling by and see a coffee shop, a hardware store, a visitor's center, a waiting room, and a dentist office. We've now made probably ten turns, with no end in sight. My knees and arms are starting to severely hurt, and I have lost all patience. We pass by a room full of plants, a production studio, a grocery store, a nursery, and a palace room with a miniature throne.

"What is this? Are you taking us in circles? It feels like this is never going to end," I say to the black cat.

"Follow me," she says.

I scoff. "We are following you. Can you give us an ETA or something?"

After about five more turns, my claustrophobia has fully set in. The feeling of panic takes over.

"I can't do this anymore! I need out!" I shout, scratching at the walls.

"Follow me," the cat says again.

"No! I'm done following you! I have to get out. I will crash through if I have to."

"You can't crash through," the cat says. "There's only one way out."

I plop down onto my back and start to cry, bracing myself against the floor to counteract the feeling of the room spinning.

"Get me out of here! I can't take it anymore."

"Which way would you go?" Pawn asks.

It feels like the hallways are endless.

"I don't know," I say through my tears.

Pawn's unexplainable composure isn't helping my panic.

"Which way do you want to go?" he asks.

I look around and come to my hands and knees again.

"Okay," I say, "Follow me," with maniacal, angry sarcasm.

The black cat hops onto my back and lies down with her head right behind mine. The arrow now points in whatever direction I'm headed. I start crawling, taking the next turn, inspecting each little cubby. I stop and take a sip out of a tiny bottle and eat a shortbread cookie off of a platter that is the size of my hand. A tan cat with bright blue eyes walks past, and I pat it on the head.

"Aren't you pretty," I say with exaggerated affection.

"Meow," it says back.

I pick up two small pillows that were perched on a couch and then little belts from a clothing rack and tie them around my knees as kneepads.

"Now my knees won't hurt. Next, we're gonna crawl," I continue.

"Pawn, get on your hands and knees and crawl. We're gonna meow until we reach the next corner, then after turning the corner, the exit will miraculously be there, and we will escape into some place way better than this…hopefully somewhere I can stand up…and hopefully, somewhere outside."

"I think you've lost it," Pawn says, but still obeying my order.

We crawl and meow our way to the next corner. Even the black cat on my back meows with us. We reach the corner, and in a moment of doubt, I close my eyes before making the turn. Pawn mutters a sound of amazement, and I open my eyes to see an end to the hallway, with a door centered just ahead.

"I'll be leaving you now. I hope you learned your lesson," the cat with the arrow says, jumping off of my back and heading in the opposite direction.

"What? Wait, who are you?" I ask, confused by the sudden change.

"I'm the arrow, of course," she says. "Take care. There is more ahead of you before you reach the end."

"That was weird," Pawn says, crawling straight toward the exit.

"The end?" I ask, pondering what she meant.

Chapter 4 — The Staff and the Stairway

I feel myself swaying, teetering, like a pendulum that's slowed down and is nearing stillness. I open my eyes to a narrow, stone walkway encapsulated by crystalline water. Inside this strange room, sparkling in all directions, a pristine tranquility rests atop the channel, which is speckled only by flattened stepping-stones and bubblegum water lilies.

Straight ahead is a statue, and I walk to the edge of the dock to get a better look. Erected atop a boulder is a mermaid, who looks toward me with a life-like quality. Perched there gracefully, she holds a golden staff. Something pulls me there, both to the water and to the statue.

I guess I'll go for a swim.

My body hits the cool water, and bubbles effervesce around me like a cherry dropped into a flute of champagne. I bob to the top, gliding my hands softly, only to realize that I'm not alone. In all directions, creatures swim alongside me, all headed in the direction of the mermaid. A gazelle swats its hoofs at the water, shifting its neck forward and back. A panther swims to my left with snout submerged and eyes piercing ahead. He looks to me, and I feel a swell of fear and awe at his glance. A banded serpent slithers across the top of the water, passing in between us. Among the others are a beaver, a tan horse with a brown mane, a lion, a sheep, a dolphin, a mink, many types of frogs and salamanders in oranges, greens, and spotted yellows, a bear and its cubs, jumping trout, and a wolf, all navigating the water, sending massive ripples out to the lily pads.

I wonder what's beneath me.

Arriving at the boulder, I climb onto a lower ledge and am greeted by the mermaid, who is, in fact, no statue. To my surprise, I am no longer inside a room, but rather I am peering at a shoreline.

The boulder, which is now out at sea, withstands the waves beneath us, and a partial rainbow glows in the distance. Beneath the mermaid, carved in the stone, are species of animals. The panther, the bear, the horse, the dolphin are all represented in the carvings.

They strike me as odd in such a location, as if some ancient royal relic had been transformed into stone, a throne fossilized there in the ocean. Just below her seat a plaque reads "Pawn the Patron."

"Hello," she says with a pleasant neutrality.

I nod, not knowing what to say to such a creature. She is the most beautiful thing that I've ever seen. The serpent from before, however, slithers right around my legs and up onto the mermaid's staff, merging with its design. The staff, which previously had one snake coiled around its base, now has two there, intertwining in helical patterns. At the top of her golden staff are two butterfly wings, framing a water lily on the zenith.

"I have a riddle for you," she says.

I recall the first Pawn from Limbo, who helped me solve the riddle before. Now, she's the one giving me a riddle. This version of Pawn is older and looks distinct in many ways from Pawn the Prodigal. That Pawn had much shorter hair and a wide smile and was closer to my age. The half-woman-half-fish before me, however, has curly, strawberry blonde hair down to her waist. Her eyes look like she's smiling, even though she's not, and she's maybe fifteen years older than me, although I can't be certain.

"Do you know who I am?" I ask.

She peers down at me with that knowing look. "Of course. I see you still have the key."

I bring my hand to my chest and notice the golden chain and key, the only thing that's been consistent through it all. Pawn the Protector springs to my mind, bringing a warm feeling to my heart.

"You know, I miss the old versions of you every time you change," I say, still admiring her beauty. "You're always just trying to stay and hang out. I've been a bit relentless in my pursuits," I add.

Her eyes twinkle back the sun's reflections on the ocean below.

"So will you solve my riddle?" she asks.

"Alright," I reply.

"For you to ascend to heaven's gate,
Finding me is in your fate.
A vertical bridge that lies in wait,
Will step you up to your next phase.
What am I?" she recites.

"Is that it?" I ask.

She nods in amusement.

"It's either a ladder or a stairway," I say.

"Come," she says, ushering me closer, still smiling as if she could burst into laughter at any second.

I move my way up the boulder, meeting her face-to-face, and notice a golden chain around her neck, not unlike mine. On the end of hers, however, dangles a spiraled shell with a keyhole at the center.

"Closer," she says, with me already just a few feet away.

I move within inches of her face. She's basically flawless.

"Do you trust me?" she asks, placing one hand on my chest and another across my eyes and nose, generating that familiar buzzing just behind my skin wherever her hands meet my body.

"Yes," I reply.

Suddenly, she grabs my shoulders and dives headfirst into the water, dragging me down…down…down…. I flounder and panic, but she's too strong. Images of sirens and sea captains and stormy oceans flood into my imagination. I fight the trajectory, scratching at her arms and feeling the threat of suffocation. With such swiftness, she has torpedoed me to a staggering depth…down…down…

Where is she taking me? Is she drowning me? Has she been tricking me all along? Pawn, should I have ever trusted you? Any of you?

"Breathe," she says. "You can breathe. It's okay. I have you."

I inhale and find that, to my surprise, I have no problem breathing underwater. I laugh out in relief. I guess I don't fully trust her yet.

Out in the distance, a large, glorious gate flashes across the ocean's bottom.

"What's that?" I ask.

"Neptune," she replies with a smile.

We near the entrance, and a cluster of ornate buildings rise up beyond the gate's obstruction. Spiraled and domed gables, opalescent and spackled materials, and golden crests decorate the structures, looming in otherworldly construction—a proper city residing just at the ocean floor. The gate itself is covered in gold and pearl adornments, looping and coiling its way around the city's perimeter as a grand and impenetrable barrier—both visibly and physically.

Pawn removes her gold chain and brings it to her lips. Moving toward the gateway's epicenter, a small imprint of a shell is etched into the space where the two great doors meet. She places the shell inside the impression and gestures me to come over.

"We need the key to enter," she says.

I remove my chain and hand it to her without hesitation, and she inserts the key into the shell. Some intricate mechanism springs into action with spirals and swirling formations shifting, like delicate gears working inside a unique apparatus.

"Here, make sure you don't lose it. We will still need it later," she says, handing me back the key.

Inside the gates, a lively town chirps with commotion. The same ethereal architecture is evident from street view, with steep pointing peaks and helical and circular decorations. The same designer appears to have worked on the city's every detail, down to the lampposts, benches, and roadways. A courtyard draws us inside, and on the perimeter, people come and go, running errands, chatting, enjoying the day. Someone leaves a bakery with a paper bag full of goods. Three women chat outside a café. A few street vendors sell produce, crafted goods, and artwork—all unlike anything I've seen before. Someone enters the post office, and another leaves. Not a single person has a face, however.

"We're not underwater anymore," I notice.

I look to Pawn and see that she now has legs instead of a tail, and a hooded garb covers her luscious hair.

"Welcome to Neptune," she says, and I detect a hint of pride in her voice.

"Remember you can't talk to the faceless. Just follow me and don't get lost," she says while picking up speed.

"Hey! Slow down!" I say, jogging to catch up with her.

"Why are we here?"

She ignores me.

"Okay…Is this version of you normally a human or a mermaid?" I ask.

Some of her curls have fallen out of the hood. If she's trying to conceal her beauty, she's not doing a great job of it.

"Remember when you were a monkey, and we meowed together like cats?" I ask, hoping to get a laugh.

She looks at me with surprise, as if I'd just said something inappropriate.

"Or…um…what about the time that we destroyed our house to free a fire-breathing dragon?"

Her eyes shift, fixating on navigating the city.

"Remember when we were in love?" I ask.

She stops in front of me. "Is everything okay? You're acting strange," she says.

I'm acting strange?

"I'd just like to know what's going on…or at least for you to talk to me," I say, feeling a heaviness in my chest.

"There's too much to explain right now. Just trust me. I'm taking you where you need to go," she says, flashing a sorrowful smile.

She grabs my shoulders again, this time leaning in for a hug. I feel the heaviness grow larger, and tears form in my eyes. Pawn has been my only companion through all of this. If it weren't for her, I would be totally lost. I'd probably still be stuck in Limbo. Her embrace feels familiar, just how each of her versions have felt familiar in some way. Is it that she reminds me of Pawn the Protector, or is it that I could be remembering her—this version of her—from a time before?

"Ok…I trust you," I say, this time saying it with more clarity.

As we walk along the street, I notice narrow waterways or trenches on either side of us. To our right, brown, murky water flows downhill, in the opposite direction of our walking. To our left is a current flowing uphill in our same direction.

We walk by a side street where the water breaks away and continues flowing. We climb the street, higher and higher, and I am winded at the steepness and pace of our trek. Pawn, on the other hand, seems perfectly in shape.

Arriving at the palace entrance, the view is spectacular. Four fountains frame the grand doors. The vein of water that traveled with us to our left flows straight into the first fountain, and a kind of valve mechanism moves the dirty water from there into the next fountain, which is closest to the left door. A brown stream flows directly from there into the palace via a passageway at ground level, then on the right side, flows out of the palace into another fountain, and then into the next, before traveling back down the street from where we came.

"That's an interesting design," I say.

We enter the grand doors and walk straight into the main hall, which is an enchanting room, with elaborate architectural details, a large circular opening in the center of the ceiling, and the continued stream around the perimeter. In the center sits a grand throne covered in etchings of sea creatures and shell formations.

A peculiar scene...

Behind is a wall of mirrors, and sitting on the throne is someone with no face. Flowing beneath the faceless's feet are long, black tendrils dancing in the air like tentacles, as if a ghost had inhabited some sheer strips of fabric and was swaying them in the breeze.

"I've returned," Pawn says, walking toward the throne.

The person doesn't move.

"I'd like to you to step aside," she presses.

"You can have anything you want," they say, still not moving.

"Thank you. Now step aside."

"Anything you want," they repeat, rising from the throne and pulling a bouquet of flowers out of thin air.

Pawn stops a few feet away.

"Anything for you, dear," they say, with tulips falling from the bouquet and landing all around the foot of the throne. Their demeanor is droopy, as are their flowers.

Pawn approaches slowly. "We're here to help," she says gently, grabbing the person's arm and lowering the bouquet.

Upon her contact, they appear to submit, lowering to their knees. Pawn, who had apparently been concealing her staff beneath her clothes, raises it and taps the top of the person's head.

Suddenly, the flowers perk up, and a face appears where there wasn't one, immediately changing to a new face, and a new one, and a new one—a series of revolving faces. The hair changes from short to long and from brown, to red, to green, to white.They change from man to woman. Their skin color changes, like someone had spun the wheel on their identity, waiting for it to land on just one. Each identity morphs into a new one, from higher cheek bones to lower, from narrow eyes to wide, from lips thin and downturned to lips plump and smiling, changing shapes rapidly. The flowers, likewise, change in variety, from roses to tulips to dandelions to daffodils to forget-me-nots to dahlias.

Finally steadying on a singular avatar, I see that their true identity was a court jester, with an appearance no less bizarre than when they had no face at all. Their hat has one peak that's white and one that's black, and their outfit is embellished with checkered designs and swirling patterns. The strangest are their eyes. The right eye is completely white, and the left eye is completely black. A wide smile forms below.

"Aha!" they shout. "It's nice to be back!"

"Thank you for watching over," Pawn says. "Would you go help the others? We have some unfinished business to attend to. I will be back soon."

The jester bows and then hands the bouquet to her, with what is now a multi-colored variety of exotic flowers. The jester then dances out of the palace doors, leaving a trail of petals in his stead.

I look at Pawn with amazement. "What just happened?"

Seeing her standing there at the foot of the throne, I see her as the queen and leader that she is.

"Come, let me show you," she says, walking over to the mirky stream running around the perimeter of the throne room. She points to the entrance where the water flows in and tells me to watch. Suddenly, the stream flowing inside changes from dirty brown to crystal clear. Pawn's already smiling eyes light up with tears of joy.

"The faceless will no longer be faceless," she replies with the same sparkle in her eyes. "Do you still have the key?"

"I do."

Pawn takes the key once again and walks over to the throne, which, similar to the city's gate, has an indentation of Pawn's shell pendant sculpted below, among the other carvings. A keyhole resides at the center.

"Wait till you see this," she says, with a kind of childlike excitement I've only seen in her previous versions.

Inserting and turning the key, that familiar whirring sound and electric buzzing fills the air around us, so strong that it quakes the ground below. The throne trembles, then dismantles, in a mechanistic series of movements before our eyes. Splitting apart, breaking down, piece by piece, realigning and then building up again in a mysterious feat of engineering, a new object appears out of the parts. A spiraling staircase emerges, reaching up…and up…all the way out of the circular window in the ceiling, defying gravity, defying logic. The stairway continues growing until I can no longer see the top. Looking straight up, I see a rainbow that arches around in a complete circle around the staircase.

"Beautiful," I say, laughing in utter amazement. "Where are we off to next?"

"Do you trust me?" Pawn asks, reaching her hand out to me. A deep admiration for her springs up in my heart, and I know that in all her versions she has brought so much comfort to me, even when I didn't know it. I don't understand a lot of things, what they mean, or why they're happening. There are a lot of things that I don't know about Pawn, but I know that I can trust her. I reach for her hand as we walk toward the staircase.

"Yes, I do."

Chapter 5 – The Book and the Truth

"Hey Pawn, look this way." I am peering through a camera lens, but an abrupt snap in awareness brings me to the present moment, like a sudden shift out of a daydream.

I was just… Where am I?

An older woman peers at me from a few feet away. Just behind her is a glass case—a display of chrysalises and cocoons—dangling in little rows across wooden boards. A sign above reads "Metamorphoses."

In her hands is an open notebook and pen, and I appear to have interrupted something.

"Sorry," I say, turning away and dropping the camera to my chest.

I instead examine the canvases on the wall in front of me. Large images of developmental phases of the human body hang boldly.

Zygote, Blastocyst, Embryo, Fetus, Infant, Toddler, Child, Adolescent, Adult, Elder.

The descriptions are helpful, because I would've never known what a blastocyst looked like.

Moving on, a sculpture in the floor's center rises up in a clumsy form, exemplifying various stages of human technology. At the base is a wheel, and all throughout the piece are gears, nuts, bolts, and machinery parts, which I couldn't begin to name. Identifiable objects include a model wagon and automobile, a model sailboat and steamboat, a vintage camera with its innards spilling out, a disposable camera, a pencil, a paintbrush, a tin can with a half-attached lid, a lightbulb, an oil lamp, a basket, and a cardboard box.

"They forgot to include a spear and a gun," Pawn says over my shoulder.

"And a speargun," I say, smirking.

"I'm glad we both made it," she replies.

"Which Pawn are you this time?" I ask.

"Pawn the Poet," she answers, gesturing at her journal.

We walk over to another part of the exhibit, and a table with two books sits plainly. One book is empty, with no lines or writing. The other book is full of designs and text. "Looks like a study of language," she says.

The book, which appears to contain some anthropological and historical assessment of language, surprisingly has some of the most interesting illustrations of the telegraph, photographs of the printing press, and an exploration of the internet's modalities of communication. The book also contains information on the Sumerian tablets, cuneiform, the Tower of Babel, Chinese writing, Egyptian hieroglyphs, and other logographs.

"You know, they'd probably love it if I brought a history book from Neptune," she says, winking at me.

I pass on to an installation of the growth stages of trees. A plaque above catches my attention, which reads "The Tree of Life." Over to the left is an animated video of the formative stages of the solar system.

Mercury shows on the screen, with a voice narrating rudimentary information about the planet.

"The planet Mercury, named after the Roman god of commerce, communication, and chance, is the smallest planet in our solar system," says the narrator.

"Hey, I think they're ready to begin," Pawn whispers, tapping me on the arm.

We walk over to where a crowd of people have formed just outside two large doors.

"What are we waiting for?" I ask.

"You'll see," she replies, putting her notebook and pen in her bag.

"Ladies and gentlemen," an announcer says over a speaker, "It is almost time to enter. An attendant is coming around to distribute the cups. Please ensure that you drink all of the contents and dispose of your cup in the trash bin provided, located below the seat in front of you. We hope you have a pleasant experience."

"What cup? Drink what contents?" I whisper to Pawn.

Suddenly, an older woman (even older than Pawn) weaves her way through the crowd, bumping into me briefly. She makes her way to the doors and slides inside, not opening wide enough to reveal what lies beyond.

The aforementioned attendants, all in silky wide-legged trousers and flowing gauzy tops, start dispersing from back to front of the crowd with serving trays. Pawn and I—who are roughly in the center of the crowd—wait to receive ours. My nerves kick in when I receive my cup and see an odd mixture inside. The liquid appears to be a cross between a tan powdery mush and a green juice. I can't say I'm dying to drink it.

The doors open, and all participants pile inside, or rather, outside. I'm not sure what I was expecting, but it certainly wasn't this. Just beyond the doors is an outdoor amphitheater etched into a canyon, with expansive rows of seating easily accommodating a few thousand people. The seats arch in semicircles, overlooking a large stage, with a massive backdrop of endless rolling hills of desert sand. The sun dips low on the horizon, casting a warm hue across the whole scene.

"Beautiful, huh? I wonder where they all came from," Pawn says.

"What do you mean?"

"All the people," she says.

The stadium is brimming with attendees, the majority of which are already seated. Our museum group pales in comparison, and as we fill the theater's back-right seating, I look to my cup and wonder what I've gotten myself into.

"Pawn, what is this?"

She quickly darts her eyes toward me with that knowing look, almost as if she's saying, "Just relax," followed by a complete ignoring of my question.

"Welcome. As you get settled into your seats, it's important for you to remember that this will be your home base for the duration of the experience."

The same older woman who slid through the museum doors is now on stage, apparently leading the presentation, which feels somewhat like a conference, but with an odd, palpable energy to the place.

A lump forms in my throat.

"If you need to get up and move, you are free to do so. Simply exit your rows and move to the side or back of the seating area. We strongly encourage, however, that you remain seated."

I look to Pawn, who is sitting forward with her back arched slightly. The cup of mysterious contents is held in one hand. The other hand is gripping her knee.

"In your cup is something very special. Contained within this mixture is a plant substance known to catalyze rapid change and open our minds to truth. You will likely experience strong shifts in your emotions and feelings, as well as a sensation that you need to express in some way. You are free to make sound, move, and do whatever feels necessary to fully express what is screaming to come out of you. The axiom of consciousness is here to penetrate the barriers of shame, reservation, and inhibition, allowing for the purest and most cathartic revelations and demonstrations. Should you need help in any way during the experience, kindly let an attendant know," the woman says.

I peer down at the dusty, sage green liquid. It's more of a sludge. I tip my cup and see that the viscosity has thickened. The smell is sweet, earthy, and pungent all at once, and at first sniff, it smells foul but with a lingering after-note with an unexpected pleasantness.

"Without further deliberation, I invite you to drink the axiom whenever you're ready," the presenter says.

Spanning the amphitheater, I see a wave of movement. As arms raise, bringing cups to lips, it looks as if an organism is moving through the air. Pawn, who has her eyes closed, takes a deep breath and then swallows in big gulps. I, on the other hand, am frozen.

Why am I not drinking it? Am I scared?

The woman continues, "We live in a world of deception, and there is a deep longing in all of us to release truth from its prison. Language—our most important technology—is the key to bridging the gaps between ourselves and others and bringing light to our shadows. Language is peculiar in that way. People once decided that certain sounds carried a particular weight and began to associate them with ideas, but language is ever evolving. Take the words 'careless' and 'carefree,' for example. The two words could easily have the same meaning, but they do not. Just the root, 'care,' has differing uses. In the case of 'careless,' to care means that you are interested in or are concerned for the wellbeing of something. To say you are careless means that you are apathetic or reckless in some way, and this has a negative connotation. Now, in the case of 'carefree,' the word 'care' is referring to one's anxieties and inhibitions and to be free of those things is usually a positive thing, is it not? To say someone is carefree means that they are upbeat or relaxed. So…what does all this say about language? It is constantly evolving…"

Come on. If I can release a dragon, carry a monkey over burning stone, and make my way out of a tiny cat maze without fully freaking out, I'm sure I can handle this.

I drink the mixture quickly, trying not to gag at its sweet, strange flavor.

Pawn is leaned back in her chair, looking dazed and vacant. Her dark brown hair looks more and more red under the tint of the sunset.

Out in the distance, the desert sand is kicked up by a gust of wind, redepositing on another dune. It's quiet here—aside from the narrator of course.

How long until the effects kick in?

The narrator continues, "And what does that say about truth? All constraints, whether self-imposed or otherwise, have no power here. You are free to say anything, to make any sound, to make any movement. These different forms of language are welcome here. There is no need to filter. There is no need to perform. There is no pressure. There are no expectations to meet. There is nowhere to be. There is nothing to do. Use the tool of language to move what is inside of you outward. You are free to express. You are free to…"

Quiet murmurings are taking place across the stadium. A vague whispering descends, but I notice that most only speak to themselves. Some have their eyes closed, making peculiar hand gestures and movements, tapping their bodies, flexing their fingers, and waving their arms and hands.

One woman nearby is hugging her arms around her body, as if she's giving herself a hug. A few people have stood, some with eyes open, speaking at full volume. Others are singing to themselves. The noise level has increased, but Pawn is slumped down in her chair looking entranced and muttering quietly. Suddenly, someone screams, and a ripple of noise cascades around the sea of participants.

"I am free!" they scream across the stadium, which gradually returns to steadier volume with time.

The sunset, which has lingered in the same spot for what feels like hours looks even redder, painting the scene with an ethereal, sepia wash. I notice a strange sensation in my mouth as a strong feeling of dryness has taken over my attention. I smack my mouth repeatedly, trying to generate moisture, unable to focus on anything else.

What is this feeling?

Licking my lips, my tongue feels hard against them. I reach in my mouth and feel a hard, bumpy texture in place of the usual soft, wet texture.

"My tongue! What…No," I say, desperately trying to understand what is happening.

I try scraping bits of it off with my nails, and I pull off a substance, similar to coal, only to find it growing right back in its place. The thickness of the rock layer feels as though it's spreading to my entire tongue, getting deeper and more rigid. A flush of adrenaline comes over me as I consider the potential causes and outcomes for this freakish phenomenon.

What do I do?

A blackness overcomes me quickly, and a feeling of dropping surges through me.

I am now on my back, looking straight up at the sky, but I don't recall lying down. I look to the left and see everyone's seating. I guess I walked over here and laid down. I wonder how long I was blacked out.

Something in the sky above me is growing larger with each second. A swarm of butterflies and moths fly straight toward me. I've never seen insects fly in such a way, almost resembling a flock of birds in formation. The winged creatures catapult straight toward my face and dive into my mouth. I can feel the fuzz on their wings and tiny feet climbing inside, and as I desperately pull them out, one after the other, they crumble into pieces. A wing, a foot, the bottom of a thorax—I carefully pull at the fragments to free myself from their attack. I pull… and tear…and tug…and gag at the disturbing sensations.

"Get out!" I scream, shuttering.

Upon removing them all, the uncomfortable stones on my tongue have disappeared. The sky still glows with the lingering sunset, only a strange pattern or grid has formed. I blink my eyes, trying to adjust them. The grid is still there, and a black circle hangs above head. I can't tell if it's a hole in the sky or a dark object. Someone on the ground in front of me has been making a lot of commotion, and I sit up to find Pawn. Propped up on her shins, she moves bizarrely with her hands and arms, almost as if gesturing in sign language. She speaks loudly and passionately in gibberish. More shocking are the giant moth wings protruding from her back. On the ground beneath her is her notebook, open and crinkled.

"Hey, your book—watch out! You'll mess it up," I say.

I crawl over and grab the journal, intending to protect it for her. She stops starkly in her tracks and looks squarely into my eyes with that inhuman glare—just as she did in Limbo as the Prodigal—but I'm not afraid of her this time.

"Do you see that?" I ask, motioning to the sky.

Her expression doesn't change, and I see that, in this version, she is weathered and worn. She seems like someone who has crazy stories to tell and could easily be jaded from a rough life but has somehow maintained her jovial demeanor.

"Carefree…You're carefree, aren't you Pawn?" I ask, grabbing her arm. "You're somehow so playful and content through it all. You are so beautiful. Every version of you has been so beautiful."

I wrap my arms around her, throwing my weight into her, and we topple over onto the earth, her wings enfolding around us.

"I want to say thank you. Having you by my side has helped me have hope! Just your presence has comforted me through it all," I say to her.

"I'm just a poet," she says with tears in her eyes and a smile that lights up the darkening sky.

"You're much more than a poet. You're Pawn the Poet," I say.

"And who are you?" she asks.

I pause. Her wide-eyed stare is hypnotic.

"You have to tell them," she says.

"Tell them what?" I ask.

"You have to say it! Tell all of them," she mumbles, looking more lucid than I've ever seen her.

"I don't have anything to tell them."

"Of course you do! Tell them!" she yells.

People over in the chairs notice Pawn's outburst. We receive strange looks, some of bewilderment and others of curiosity, and one participant starts to repeat the phrase.

"Tell them…Tell them…" he repeats.

Some of the people around him take notice and start mirroring his repetition.

"Tell them…Tell them…" they say.

"You have to just say it. Tell them! Tell them!" Pawn joins in on the choir of her own creation.

I feel a surge of excitement rising up from the pit of my stomach, up into my chest and throat. The chant has spread across the stadium and is growing in volume as more join in.

"Tell them! Tell them! Tell them!"

"They don't even know what they're saying," I say to Pawn.

"So what? Whatever you need to say, you have to let it be heard," she says.

The light of the sun has almost made its way past the horizon. The reddish hue has softened into a slightly bluer one. I stand and see a sea of people, standing and chanting, and the pattern on the sky has extended out into the crowd.

Okay. I will.

I start to walk downhill, passing row after row. Some of the attendees have started harmonizing with the chant, and an echo rings out, booming a heavenly chorus across the theater. Deep bass voices and beautiful sopranos intermingle and weave together. People sway and dance.

The energy is palpable, sending chills all the way up my spine and down my arms.

"Tell them. Tell them," they sing.

The stage is empty. The narrator has gone, and I feel a rising sensation up from the core of my being. I reach the stage and walk right up the steps, headed toward the spotlight, which glares onto a microphone stand right in the center. Thousands of eyes are on me. I see their tussled hair and disheveled clothing, all of them absorbed in the song. How could they not be? The sound of them all is truly divine. Many of them look at me with wide eyes, waiting for me to join them. I step up to the microphone, clutching Pawn's journal close to me.

What barriers have lived inside of me for so long? What have I stifled? What is in there screaming to be expressed?

The hole in the sky has widened. The grid looks even more prominent. It moves and swirls and thwarts the image. I can no longer see them or hear them. There is only a sea of sound and soft light.

I open my mouth and brace myself against the thunder—against what will spill out of me and reverberate across the whole wide expanse.

From my lips, the sound springs forth.

"I have something to say!"

Chapter 6 — The Pearl and the Dream

"I know you're there! Why are you following me?" I shout across the dimming forest.

Just moments ago, an apparition briefly floated by in my peripheral vision. The towering hemlocks obstruct most incoming light from imminent dusk, which faintly illuminates the undergrowth with a faint purplish glow. There is no sign of movement.

Could I have imagined it?

I turn around and walk fearfully in the opposite direction, wishing that I had eyes in the back of my head. The pressing feeling of a dark spirit at my heels sends a quivering energy up my tail bone and spine. I've been walking for hours.

Why am I in the woods? Where am I going?

My last memory of the amphitheater abruptly halts into blackness. It's just me in this forest and whatever hunts me. I thought Pawn would have shown up by now.

Suddenly, I see something narrow and black float through the air, disappearing behind a tree, with nothing reappearing on the other side.

I definitely didn't imagine that… Was that a snake?

It's true that when you have no presumed destination and nothing drawing you closer, one of the only things that really propels you forward is fear. Had I not seen the mysterious floating and disappearing act, I might have decided to lie down in the dirt and quit my wandering. There is nowhere for me to get to, after all, and I might as well not waste the energy. I back away even though the floating object has vacated view.

No, a snake wouldn't make sense. I've been getting the feeling that I'm being followed. A snake wouldn't follow me… Would it?

I recall the serpent that attacked me in the garden that day. I guess I can't assume anything here, especially in a world of talking monkey boys and magically appearing doorways. Anyway, it wouldn't be the first time that I've seen a floating snake.

Walking in any opposing direction, I notice a pair of eyes peeking out from behind a tree. They are not just any eyes. Glowing amber orbs with prominent pupils pierce the distance. A large head inquisitively reveals itself from behind a tree, and I can see its full, dark face—as black as space.

Edging out of concealment, a panther slowly walks toward me, patting down the forest floor quietly with its padded feet. Everything in me is frozen in place. My vision narrows. My heart beats aggressively. My ears perk up in sharp attention.

Move! Don't just stand there.

Something in my impulse to freeze passes, allowing my flight impulse to win over. I dart away as fast as I can, expecting to be snatched in a second. Nothing holds my body back now. I am running so fast that it feels like my weight in gravity has lessened. I can feel the panther's teeth gnashing my back, its hot breath prickling the hairs up my body. I run so fast that I fall, and in falling, I realize that the panther is not chasing me. Exhaustion sets in as well as the need to vomit. I crawl next to a standing root system of a fallen tree and let it shelter me from view.

I stand no chance against this thing. It must be toying with me.

My breath deepens as I try to collect myself in the face of the looming threat. I recall the time when I found myself swimming alongside a variety of creatures, one of which being a black panther.

Why am I so afraid now? It never attacked me then. I wasn't even that scared.

Sweat drips down my upper lip, and I wipe it away, realizing I have no food or water. There's nothing I can do. I will die eventually, even if the panther doesn't get me.

I suppose Pawn isn't coming, and I don't know how to escape this forest. The memory of the small black cat enters my mind.

"There is more ahead of you before you reach the end," she said.

Is this really the end for me? What a strange ride it has been.

I think back to Limbo—where it all started. Flashes of the dark hallway enter my mind.

"Welcome to your dreams," the entrance said.

My longing for Pawn increases. In all the other places I've been, she—or he—shows up quickly for me.

Is this all really just a big dream? It doesn't feel like a dream…I can't say that any of this is normal either. Shouldn't I just wake up then?

The panther emerges from behind a thin tree, its body manifesting from nowhere, like a glitch in a game. I run a short distance to once again attempt evasion, but I stop in my tracks. If this is just a series of dreams, I have no need to run. I will wake up the second it kills me. If I'm wrong about this being a dream, at least I won't be prolonging the inevitable. I turn around and face the terror, my body buzzing with adrenaline.

"Come and get me!" I yell.

Slow signs of movement are made as the panther advances toward me. Frustration boils to the surface.

What was the point of all of this? I still don't know who Pawn really is. I have no answers. I never arrived to wherever this was leading.

The two possibilities—to wake up or to die—both sadden me, even knowing that waking up would feel like the escape I've really been looking for or the attainment of whatever I've been seeking. Part of me still wishes that Pawn will swing in and save the day somehow.

"Come on!" I scream.

For a moment, it pauses, motionless, postponing its prowling urges, but then resuming with head low and fixed, its shoulders glide up and down, readying itself to pounce. Its eyes glow with a human-like intelligence.

Pure power, you are.

I ready myself for death—or for waking up—but, before my eyes, the panther transforms. Balancing upright briefly, his body changes into that of a man's, with his head and upper torso staying the same.

I stand frozen, unable to remove my gaze from him as he steps closer, his presence enveloping me like a shadow. Accepting the peculiar violence to come, I stand slack, my feet planted firmly on the Earth, my attention focused on the creature in front of me. The amber hue of his eyes has captivated me. I cannot look away from the deep, translucent intensity of his gaze.

They look so human…They look so familiar…

"Pawn?" I ask.

I offer no resistance as he reaches out a hand and touches my face.

"What the hell!" I say, swatting away his hand. "Why did you scare me like that?"

With his eyes still shining hypnotically, I manage to look away briefly, but something sucks me right back in. I see the familiar look in him—the look they all have. In this moment, I see him, beyond all his variations.

"Focus," he says.

"On what?" I ask.

He stands just inches away. "Focus," he repeats.

I obey and peer straight into his eyes with unwavering attention. They hold me, like someone who catches you as you faint. I can feel the weight of my focus falling on him and him holding it steadfastly. The intensity grows, and that faint whirring sound and buzzing manifests from nowhere. My vision narrows, and he places his hands on the base of my skull and neck, creating an intense electric sensation.

Eyes…all I can see are his eyes.

He bring his hands up and around my face, resting them over my eyes and forehead. The vibration penetrates into my skull, as if my brain has been plugged into an electrical outlet. In the darkness of my mind, a vision of a white sphere spins in front of me, with geometric patterns etched into its surface. It hangs there, spinning slowly, only then to suddenly fly straight into my forehead. Then, everything goes black.

I open my eyes to an open field. Pawn must have found a clearing in the trees, although I don't see any trees in the vicinity. I peer around and find him standing right behind me.

"Pawn, what's going on? Just tell me," I plead.

The half-panther-half-man ignores me and stares up at the sky.

"Who are you?" I ask.

"I'm the Prophet," he says, not wavering his concentration.

"What's going on? Please. I'm tired of wondering. Am I dreaming?"

The words spill out with tears welling up in my eyes. I step in front of him, grabbing his shoulders.

"What's happening? Please! I know you know something. Have I gone mad? Do I need to wake up?"

"What makes you think this is a dream?" he asks, looking at me finally.

"I…It said in Limbo…'Welcome to your dreams,'" I say.

I can't ascertain his expression. He is a cat, after all.

"Please. Don't be so mysterious. I can't take it anymore. I feel like I'm going crazy. Where is everyone? Why is it just me and you? Who are you? Why do you change? Why do we wake up somewhere new? Why is everything so strange?" I ask sloppily, grabbing his thick shoulders.

"Did you see the pearl?" He asks flatly.

Light flashes across the sky, and Pawn stares with wide eyes at the sky behind me. I turn around to see an image more spectacular than I have ever seen. A massive swirling vortex of vibrant celestial bodies, planets, rings, asteroids, and empty space hang there in every color, spiraling slowly in the most exuberant show of hues and radiance. Spiraling clockwise, planets of every shape and size spin on their axes, their surfaces adorned in crimson, sapphire, emerald, magenta, teal, and colors I've never known existed. It is a miraculous picture of entire worlds and solar systems spinning. It's as though I'm looking into the central mind of the universe.

"Beautiful," is all I can mutter under my breath.

"Yes. It's a double helix," Pawn says, his eyes reflecting the kaleidoscope colors. "Here, look," he says, pointing to a planet straight above us, a solid, icy blue sphere.

"Where are we?" I ask.

I notice that familiar buzzing radiating throughout my whole body.

"Pawn, what's happening?" I plead.

The feeling of an electrical current energizes my body from head to toe, permeating my every cell. In a forceful combination of pleasure and pain, I feel myself levitate off the ground, and a white light encompasses me in an indescribable sensation.

I scream in agony and ecstasy as the cosmic scene fades into a field of white light.

Chapter 7 – The Room and the Void

Floating here in space, I wonder... What if this is all there is—the constant change, continual searching and movement, with never a final arrival or fulfillment? What if things are always strange, and the places are always new? What if I'll always be wondering if this is a dream, existing in the odd occurrences that happen between waking and sleeping and sleeping and waking? I don't want to consider it.

"I'm glad we both made it," Pawn says,

The Earth hangs below, suspended in the void. A black backdrop is painted by a rotating sphere of blue and green.

"Pawn, I'm tired. When will it end?"

The being looking back at me is hardly a person. They glow like a small star, light obscuring any discernible features. The lines of human form are blurred and blended, but despite that, the presence is unmistakable. They are Pawn.

"What exactly do you want to end?" they ask.

"I...want to get where we're going. I don't want to search anymore," I say.

The ball of light hovers in front of me.

"Is the adventure really so bad?" they ask.

I look out to space, the twinkling sky, and the spinning planet beneath me. I haven't considered it as an adventure.

"No…but something is still missing. Something's off," I say.

From the light emits no sound, no reply.

"Where are the others? Who are you? Who am I? What are we doing? It just feels like I'm stuck in a loop," I continue.

"What's the loop?" they ask.

"The loop…The loop is…I just begin somewhere. I search for something, then it ends, and then a new mission begins. I'm right back to the beginning...again. The loop never ends. It's exhausting."

"What if that's all there is?" they reply.

A pause briefly settles in the air. "No, I don't like that," I say.

"Okay. Let's change that."

In a blink, the Earth and stars disappear, along with Pawn's light. I am floating in pure darkness. Me and the void: That's all there is.

"Is this what you want? Do you feel complete now?" Pawn asks.

The darkness?

"No…I don't want to be alone! I don't want there to be nothing."

"Then you should turn on the light," they say.

I feel an object appear in my hands, just as the box did when I entered Limbo—only this time, the rectangular shape has a protrusion of sorts.

Turn on the light…

I flick the switch, and now I'm in a white room—with no visible windows, doors, objects, or color in the space. It's just a white room. I look to my left and see Pawn, only that familiar look, that knowing look, sits behind a face I recognize all too well.

"Who are you?" I ask.

"I'm Pawn."

"No! Tell me really. Be honest. Who is Pawn?"

A new and strange expression falls on their face.

"Okay…I'm Pawn the Pure," they say, changing appearances to that angelic creature bathed in white light. "I'm Pawn the Paragon," they say, changing again. "I'm Pawn the Philosopher, the Performer, the Pursuer, the Provocateur," they go on, changing identities with each proclamation. "The Protege, the Prodigy, the Professor, the Proclaimer. I'm Pawn the Paladin and the Patriot, the Phantom, the Psychopomp, the Pinnacle. I'm Pawn the Paradox… I'm all of it. I'm you," they say, finally landing back on the appearance I know so well, the one I saw in the mirror when first arriving in Limbo.

Something appears on the wall ahead. A golden frame filled with a perfect glass surface hangs there.

"Look," Pawn says, gesturing to the mirror.

I walk over and look inside, first seeing myself, but then an image manifests, as if I'm watching a movie. I am walking into a darkened corridor toward a rotating door. Flipped about like a leaf in the wind, I land in a small room with two doorways, one exuding light and color, and the other a total darkness.

"Where am I now?" I ask.

"Limbo. You're always in Limbo," Pawn says. "What if that's all there is? Is that so bad?"

I try to mask my disappointment.

"And this room too? This place feels different," I say.

"You should've seen it before. It was a mess," they reply with a smile.

I look around at the purely white surface. Not even a crumb is visible. *A mess?*

"We've been cleaning it up during out little adventures," they say, moving around the room. "Now that the filth is gone, we get to fill it with whatever we like. We can come here anytime, and we can do whatever we want…create whatever we want. It's a blank page, but it's still Limbo. You're always in Limbo, so you better make friends with it."

I…am stuck here.

"Is the adventure really so bad? Would going on be worth it? Are you really so determined to come to a plateau?" Pawn asks, noticing my displeasure.

Smiling faintly at the question, memories flash across my mind and remind me of the answer.

Yes…It is worth it… Even during the unpleasant parts I have still wanted to go on.

"I didn't really stop to enjoy it very often. If I'm really stuck in this dream… even if I'm stuck here… Yes, it is worth it!" I decide.

Pawn pauses, and the scene on the mirror stops as well.

"What if you're awake or asleep? What does it change?"

"Change? Nothing, I suppose," I reply with a bit of doubt.

"Does it make you less free? Would you change your behavior?"

"I suppose that I would try to wake up if I was asleep," I reply.

"Why?"

"Because of other people…I don't want to be alone. I want to experience others, and for others to experience me," I say.

"Do the people in your dreams feel less real? Don't you know that you're never alone?"

A feeling of loyalty and admiration for Pawn surfaces in me.

"You have been with me all this time," I say, smiling.

Pawn nods. "How would you ever know if things are real or not real?"

"I suppose that I can't."

They smile at me. I'm finally coming to understand.

"So…you're awake or you're asleep. You can't know, and what difference does it make? The limitations don't change. Can you be happy? Can you stop always looking for an escape route? Is this enough? Can it all be enough?"

I stare at the mirror with tears streaming out of me, the reflection opening my reservoir of emotions. Deeper acceptance softens my core.

"And you're me? You're just me…All this time?"

I nod, the reflections echoing my knowing.

"So…this isn't the end?" I ask.

"Not quite."

"Where do I go from here?"

"Limbo, of course."

PART 2
The Earth

Air

Spiritus Mundi

The sound of a subtle wind aborescently weaves,
Caressing the canopy of a thousand assorted greens,
Harmonies of grass blades, branches, and leaves.
I do not see the route but hear its passage
And feel the skyward reprieve.

I know the sound like submersion in rolling waves,
The edge of abyss, the tidal crashes and caves,
Of the turning of tandem galaxies in contested claves,
Matter etheric yet ferocious, nebulaic calamities,
Helical oscillations as cosmic bodies misbehave.

Sounds of the vitae of the masses,
Both of uniformity and aberration,
A seraphic view of mortal lifeblood variation,
Of the flighted fluttering abstracted murmurations,
Of the humming of nimble bees and ladybug wings,
The constant changing on a whimsy of stations,
Darting in a delicate, dynamic array,
Swarming and syncopating on their way.

Ensconced in the sounds of her choir, which require quiet,
She serenades me sweetly in hushed and hummed harmonies,
Soul in utter absorption
In the Mundi Mother.

Arctornis

I am a messy changling.
I am the pupa in the cocoon,
The little fetus in the womb,
New limbs morphing out of old,
Sinewy shapes from the mold,
Mighty muscle and bone,
From dust to dust.

The prior home was temporary.
The shedded skins lay a trail behind,
New scales glimmering in a perfect line.
I remember but won't look back,
Old kingdoms soon turned to ash,
Once flightless to winged thorax,
From dawn to dusk.

> (Will you die a million times?
> Trading bodies, from one shape to the next?
> What exists to forever hold your weight?
> The process.)

Breath Of Life

When I was young, I almost drowned,
And as I sunk there, thrashing around,
From my wetted lips escaped a gurgling sound.

Right there at the surface, floundering and frantic,
In my self-inflicted turbulence in this suburban Atlantic,
I was merely a nostril length away from the breath of life!

To die there—
What a waste it would've been—
Dare I say, a sin,
In that apartment complex chlorine.

A young woman took notice and was alarmed.
She saved me, that sunny day, from imminent harm,
Grabbing me up by my floaty-cladded arm.

Upon asking, "Are you okay?" kindly,
I replied, "Yes, ma'am," politely,
And she told me I didn't need to call her ma'am.

What a brief memory there submerged in my mind,
And I wonder if she remembers my moment of fright,
How she lifted me above my self-made waves.

Or has she forgotten her shining armor,
(Which curiously resembled swimming attire)
That made all the difference in this life of mine?

Cloud Crown

I could write of love,
But I was destined for trickery.
Many people prefer a simpler message
Or at least one stated differently.
"Get on with it," they'd say,
And then move on with their day,
Feeling clever in the knowing
They were given something with ease,
And with which they could relate.

I am far more drawn to riddles and mazes,
Or something spoken elaborately, in a subtle way,
Or in something that stirs up a current in me.
"Startle me into passion!" I'd say.
I am young and tired of every latest fashion.

I have been told many times
That the clouds stack around my head like a crown,
An insult I've grown to love as compliment.
I wish before that I would've known my nature.

So climb with me up the ladder
Madder than a hatter...
Are you ready to explore?
We will spell out the atoms of our souls
In this fun little soirée,
Where every truth is a trick,
And every tragedy is for play.

The current messages are normal,
And tomorrow they'll be bizarre,
But don't fret with the alterations.
You're everything they said you are and more.

You are abysmal, cataclysmal, everlasting darkness.
You are a melancholic melodrama plagued by madness.
You are sitting atop the mountain on your golden throne.
You are beauty and purity itself
In robes holy white and adorned.

The current you is normal.
Tomorrow, you'll be bizarre.
Every day, you're something new.
Every day, you are reborn.

Facing Starlight

My heart was a hopeful sunrise,
With red flames in my forlorn blue eyes,
Upon us meeting.

A warmth, steady and gold, was shone,
And now I won't face sunset alone,
In your presence here.

I'll be glad the day was spent with you,
As the clock shows us the darkest blue,
When the starlight comes.

Path of Totality

A young woman marching toward middle age—
With (somewhere in there) a fear uncaged—
Is still afraid of the dark.

Sitting there in a visual void—
With merely a few minutes toiled to keep her poise—
She faces shadows unseen.

Comfort comes with a new thought
And diverts the doubt through a glimmer fought.
A little light shines.

Somewhere (if not here) is the light of day
And it reminds her that darkness does not stay.
All things come to an end.

Paper Bullets Have Wings

Too many things wouldn't fly with you,
So I flew away.
There's an edge you were clinging to,
To resist the falling.

I couldn't be the sturdy stone
Because I'm too soft.
You plucked my feathers when alone,
Wings too weak for two.

I hope it was worth it—
That hefty price in the steep chasm,
And that you crawl out, truly,
And that you don't forget to notice
The city you built and burned at the very edge,
Parading and proclaiming,
"I will do great things."

But I can't dance when armored up for battle.
Your requests for both silence and music were futile.
Instead I left screaming,
"I will do great things,"
Vowing to give you neither.

I hope you work the land
And break the bread
And shape the scape
To your mind's silent plans,
That your cup is filled
And your lot in life is received
As I aim ahead and don't look back,
As I do great things.

Earth

The Promised Land

Oh, how I crave it!
To feel feet bare on the ridged pathways,
To let the stone rub raw at the soles.
Let the twigs twist in penetrated lacerations.
Let the damp moss soothe and dirty the wounds.
Open my skin to the messages of the masses,
Those found only in my raptured solitude.

Breathe into my veins.
My tendons and ligaments will bore down into the clays.
Sweet songs of the trees—
I hope to never lose the language of them
And to never forget the names of each,
The simplest dialect with only sounds of truth.

My quiet friends—
They speak through silent intuitions.
I hear them faintly but clearer in mind
Than any words shouted.
I respond to them in romantic whispers.
"I am yours" to the river,
To fling myself into you from the highest peak
And be carried downstream.
"I belong among you all" to the knotted roots,
To feel the pebbles and smell the soil
As I fade into the background.

They sing back to me
As a choir to this solo congregation,
Words meant only for me.
"I have come for what is mine."

Substance of the Forest

Blast off!
When the colors and senses are beyond all description,
Listen.
When the symbols and fractals are detailed and endless,
Defenseless.
When you climb to such heights you can see the whole structure,
The Sculptor.
When you beg it to end but it had no beginning,
Patience.
When the matter created is disintegrated,
Spacious.
When you sit with the chaos in what is called nothing,
Something.
When you are the rope tying realms and dimensions,
Mending.
When you cry all your tears and realize they're endless,
Rest.
When you are the bringer, the vessel for message,
Collect.
When divinity hides, play with the concepts,
A Quest.
When you arrive at the ultimate and realize it's you,
Truth.

Narcissus' Garden

I watch you as you glaze your lips
With some clear-as-glass sticky paste,
Pink-flavored in a petroleum base
In Poison Berry, the latest shade,
As if they weren't already plump.

What an exquisite chemical concoction—
Those oval nails hardened in acrylic—
In your personal favorite, the glittery option,
Fooling us all with your stunning deception,
In so many names and uses for artifice.

Skin glowing not from sun nor shine,
But from a bottle, a powder, a spray
In red #40 and yellow #5...
The veil of beauty.

Someday all the glitter will reach our brains,
Thanks to the gifts from (you know the ones)
Those cosmetic chains,
As a cost-effective, potent antidepressant,
In plastic picnics lit by artificial fluorescence,
With appetizers not even the worms would eat.

When discussing our options, costly or affordable,
Do we forget in our apathy that we are mortal?
Surely that is to be considered in our cost-benefit analysis,
But I guess the price of beauty has simply skyrocketed.

Orange and Green

I'm learning to open my heart again,
But those things we said that rainy weekend
Were like ricocheting ping-pong balls
Against two parallel, opposing walls.
We have always been at a crossroads,
Paths perpendicular, fighting the facts.

As I stood there and watched it rain down your cheeks,
I realized I had never seen you cry.
Your mouth was downturned and quivering this time,
And though I couldn't muster up a fuck, I tried.

Your pointed fingers and drooping face invoke nothing in me.
So many times, I was in your shoes, battered by heartache,
And I stood squarely there in front of you,
Or sat doubled over in a chair,
Or crouched in a corner of the kitchen,
Or collapsed beneath a tree in open air,
Or begged for you and reached,
And from you received no sympathy.

Now my efforts left an imprint that you can't escape.
My fingerprints are stamped
All in the orange and green wall paint.
The ugly familiar, a well-known stranger,
An old home that almost crushed me while crumbling.

So I'll never go there again.
I will never sit in that spot.
The moss on the stones will rot,
And I will miss it all.
That home is lost.
The places I thought were constant were not.
It's over.

Dead Flowers

Dead flowers in a vase on the coffee table,
And a fire is lit and devouring.
You are there, dabbling on the strings,
Singing sweet nothings.

Will I remember?

The type of flowers and the color of vase?
The etching on the wooden mantle?
The lyrics of the song you sing?
What notes you hit?
What we ate for dinner and poured to drink?
Those invisible things that
Push and pull people together
And back away again?
I don't know them,
And they don't matter to me.

Those things, forgotten and dead,
Like how we arrived,
And why we stayed,
The day of departure,
The love that was lost,
And the misdeeds we forgave?

They are there, inside the borders of a snapshot
Of you playing forever love.
Forever.

The Boy in the Sandbox

I know a boy.
To him, life is a sandbox.

His fun is rough but takes no toll,
When building castles and digging holes,
In a self-made world like his.

Instead of sand, it is rich soil,
And there his work is play, not toil,
Which is how it should be.

Although my petals and leaves are wilted,
I peer in with my head tilted,
Doubt overridden by allure.

My cynical, weary, and sullen aim
Doesn't prohibit me from playing the game
With the boy in the sandbox.

His sudden professing of invitation
Startles me with deep, hidden elation.
How could I say no?

Upon my "Yes," he smiles wickedly,
Replying on impulse, "Make a mess with me."
He digs a hole, and I jump in.

He etches words at my roots:
"Love is not a game, and life's play is the pursuit."
I ponder it as a truth.

He rewards himself, so I do, too.
I say to him, "I'm rewarding myself with you,"
As I remember how to love and play.

Fingers to fertilizer, mind to matter,
Safe in his soil with the seeds he scatters,
A girl in the sandbox.

So he makes room for me to grow,
Pruning and watering me in overflow.
I bask in his love like a flower in the sun.

Calamus (Caveman Calls)

What do the trees say?
And the green plants that speckle the way?
The calamus? The spearmint? The sweetgrass?
Speak it, sir. Speak it loudly.
I should know their words by your lips.

What do the wolves say?
The tiny creatures that move about?
The hummingbird? The dragonfly?
The centipedes beneath your tread?

Shall we list them all, my love?
To the moss! To the rocks! To the dirt!
Tell me! Tell me it all!
Of foxes and beavers! Of deer and cats!
Of the wind and air and sun!
My love, what could have been and still could be?
He who speaks their language, what does he say?
He who builds of them and for them all?
He who knows the messages of the path?
The magician, the alchemist, the caveman?

Of his words, I would love sincere whispers,
In close and prophetic intimacies,
But I know he would wish to yell the message.
I say, "In blaring echoes as a barbarian
Over the canyons of cavernous distance, shout it out!
I will not forget those things you say
And what is told to me.
I will not forget what could have been and still could be."

Fire

In Heat

Things I saw alone—
Missing you in pairs of two—
While you were not home.

Urges for mating—
Dragonflies copulating—
During hot summer.

Two ducks on the pond—
One green head, one speckled blonde—
Drift in harmony.

Evergreen contrasts—
Paired cardinals, red and brown—
In snowy forecasts.

Sparkling bits of green—
Iridescent dancing wings—
Butterflies mid-air.

Two benches facing—
I, on one and listening—
To my own longing.

Fire Worship

I want.

A flame too hot—
It pops and coils unpredictably.
Something unsuspecting it will eat up next.

An initial attraction—
Too elusive, incorporeal,
A slippery thing, so sadly unfixed.

To worship it with all sincerity—
Is to watch it devour
With violence, in silence, with the deepest passivity,
(But not in superficiality),
And to not command it to go,
But to know it will go when it desires.

And should you be a contained chaos,
Poised in the face of all your passions,
Should you stare your lover in the eye
And choose to look away for fear of wanting,
Should you crave so amorphously
That your body writhes at the intensity
Of what screeches inside to escape,
You will know that what is worthy of worship
Is bewildering and crazen,
Impermanent...
And the worship is as well, but is still needed.
Oh, how it's needed!

So don't armor up with your shyness.
It wants to meet you there
And gobble you up in its mightiness.

Pardon the severity of mind,
Pardon the heights of excitement,
Pardon the low, guttural roar,
Pardon, pardon, pardon...
Until it is there no more.

Is that your form of worship?

It is not mine.
My desires and pleasures—I will claim and cling to them,
Like a hysteric screaming for bed-rested freedom.
Because the objects are never graspable.
It is in me that it arises and is gratified.
Let me scream it to the clouds,
Pound it into pavement and stone.

I will worship the flame for all my days,
For all my life,
Forevermore.

Temazcal

A hut in mud, a black circle room—
It is what they call the "Great Earth Womb."
Songs and sobs will begin soon,
A filthy hole, an obscure new moon.

Doors one, two, three, and four,
With the flame at the deepest core,
A longing and hope to be restored,
Reached only through what must be mourned.

Begins door one—the fire we stoked...
Then door two—to the water, we spoke...
Door three—of air and of herbal smoke...
Door four—of earth whose heart we hold...

A woman sat at the foot of the door,
While sweltering heat seeped into our pores.
The only solace was the cool, mud floor,
But I—silent and wanting more.

"Sisters, sisters, I've known you, always."
She digs her fingers into blackened clays.
"For you, I have something I wish to say."
My ears erect to hear her pray.

"Ladies, ladies, we must have land,"
Pounding the ground with a sharp, firm hand.
"For this Earth, we must stand!"
In a tone close to a reprimand.

"When you go home, how will you thrive?
How much will you take of what She provides?
Will you return and keep Her alive?
I plead with you to make it right!"

As I sat harshly, ass to the clay,
A fevered passion arose that day.
An energy awakened from down below,
And traveled into my heart, head, and throat.

A great wail escaped!
A strange, guttural, wicked emote.
The four doors were then closed.
Possessed with a message and here, I wrote.

Sunshine Youth

Sunshine youth under a heavy blanket,
Dense fog clouding the beams.
"I was only seventeen," my anthem rings.
Afraid of the worst—to be alone—
Learned fears pre-birth,
Acting out the story.

In my reverie, I whisper,
"What a shame."
In my world,
People approach smiling.

On the piece of paper caught in my eye
Was a request to meet at first sunlight.
A note to self:
"Greet me how you should greet the day—
Gleaming with a hopeful grin on your face."

Red Shoes

They wear swords against their waists,
Jewels around their necks,
Red shoes upon their feet,
And crowns atop their heads.

We know the way, but they lead the people.
We dodge their advances and attacks.
They dance with gods and devils,
While we carry the flame to the wax.

They work only to steal the goods
And know where to get much more,
But they will be rightly punished
When we take back what is ours.

Leonurus Cardiaca

Listen when none speak
To the little spirits.
Remember their language
Through a deep silence.

This one tastes bitter,
But she feels so sweet.
Dainty yet ferocious,
She cools your hot and sweaty brow
While you're climbing the rugged peak,
With a sharpness fit to cut the muck,
And an effect I hope to keep.

She reminds you
That no one is your master,
And everyone's your teacher,
To not forget your power,
That you are your own leader,
To not lose your hope or wits,
When searching for the meaning,
To not miss the point,
When fixating on the reasons.
To soften in the center,
And let the energy run free,
To release the holding,
And allow yourself to grieve.

Listen when none speak,
To her most gentle song.
She smooths the edges when you're prickled and tired,
And with a hug, she tells you that your heart is strong,
Soothes your nerves and calms the raging fire.

When your will is weak like your spine,
And your heart aches down to the floor,
She assists you with a straight stance
And forms a straight line in your core.
She is a mother with magic.
With a big hug, she knows how to cure.

The lion heart
Helps you free fall from the nest
But only when you're ready.

She says,
"You are brave.
Through all your resilience and resistance,
You are brave.
With each heartbeat, you defy the odds.
You are brave."

The Porcelain Dragon

He calls me "baby doll" when I sleep,
An endearment thoughtlessly given,
Diverging from the waking vacancy,
When eyes are open,
And he calls me nothing,
No doting words or niceties.

Hushed breathing brings him peace,
Unlike my noisy and impassioned speech.
My head back slack and eyes fluttering
Contrasts the inquisitive brow and mind discerning.
"Baby doll"—an object so nonchallenging
Which comes alive the second you leave.

A doll come to life is a scary thing!
A snarling monster cloaked as figurine,
With appearance as fair, fragile, defenseless, weak,
Is a fretful ploy masking jagged teeth,
So shouldn't he be silent so as not to wake me?

Water

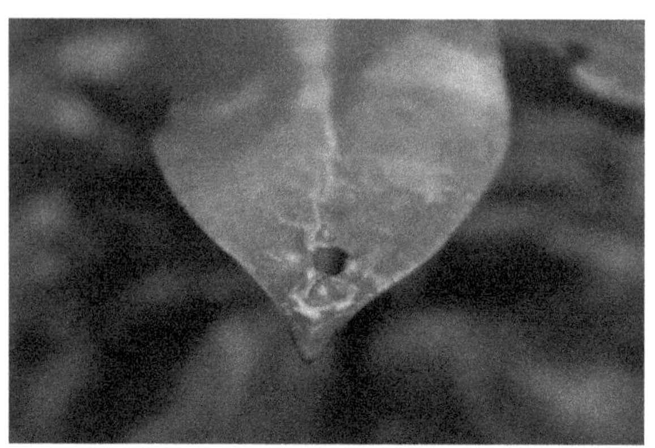

Those Storms

Those storms—
They are rolling in...
Messages messages messages messages
And I will listen.

Because who am I
To deny them?
They carry a fine weight, an admirable density,
So that tranquility emerges clearer and lighter than before.

A potion pours over the dry land,
A mundane mind saturated by sudden realizations,
Recollections streaming down from the heavens.
It's the only water I've ever known,
A shock to the system,
A sudden satiation.
I must listen to and allow,
The pitter-patter pissing all over my illusions.

The more I fight for sunshine,
The greater the storm needed.
When all is dissolved—
Beyond the inner squeals and outer squalls—
There is only silence.

Float

When I was small, I floated,
Soft and fragile and tender,
Bound up in a castle, unfree,
Inside a tiny, translucent prison.
I was shielded, sheltered, blinded,
And in growing bored, I resisted.
The mountains seemed like toy-hills,
The weights silly in comparison,
And in my increase, the tank spilled over,
Leaving me with the grandest decision:
Will I stay here and be squished inside?
Or leave in a devastation, a flood?
And even in my wavering, I knew
There was no more room for me to hide.

When I was small, I floated,
Everything assumed, everything granted.
All the mountains were climbable.
All the weights had been carried before.
All the waters had been treaded,
And I was never too far from the shore.
I didn't know of the sharks
Or the great swelling waves.
I didn't know of the ships capsized,
Or the others who were never saved.
I didn't know just how many colors of coral existed!
I had never seen glimmering schools of fish,
And now I swim with a bit of ease,
Grateful that I persisted.

A Frog on a Lily Pad

I am a frog on a lily pad.
I swim. I eat. I sit—
Jolly, warm, and fat—
And so, I know
Nothing is wrong.

I am a fly on the frog's head.
I will be discovered soon, and then dead!
But not yet, so there's no need to dread,
And so, I know
Nothing is wrong.

I am the lily pad down below.
I absorb the sun and grow.
One thing I do well is float,
And so, I know
Nothing is wrong.

I am the water and the dew,
The sun, clouds, and sky so blue,
The earth below and the whole view,
And so, I know
Nothing is wrong.

I am a human observing on the bank,
The frog and fly and lily on the lake.
A piece of the scene, and here I'll stay,
And so, I know
Nothing is wrong.

When Water Is Gold

When water is gold,
Our streams will be pure,
Teaching us how to endure,
Turning poisons into nutrients.

When water is gold,
We will follow the water's command,
And neither conquer nor own the land,
The voracious flame of greed being dampened.

When water is gold,
We will ask before we take.
Knowing when to carve rigid stone into a pathway,
And when to lead with a soft heart.

Medicine Man

Lay your remedies on me.
My body longs for your medicine.
I am starving.
I sip up every last drop.
Any action of yours is an elixir to me,
Fevered to be fixed.
You taught me how to crave
And trust each treatment you gave,
So lay them on me, medicine man.

Lay your remedies on me.
My body longs for your medicine
In true hysteric fashion.
I follow the prescriptions,
The first of which is bed rest,
The last—right friction.
I notice your details,
Each movement in effortless precision,
So lay them on me, medicine man.

At the corners of the creek
(Which I'm sure have known others),
We became one with the waters.

Lay your remedy on me.
I long for it, the panacea.
If I pull away, squeeze tighter.
If I look away, step back into view.
When I doubt, show me pure faith.
Fall on me with all your weight.
Lay it on me, medicine man.

The Wave Wrangler and a Little Panic

Everyday stirs up
A little Panic.
A little Panic a day
Requests to join Joy at the bay.
But Joy likes clear waters,
And Panic brings a darkness.

And me? I'm the Wave Wrangler.
That is my profession.
In the waters of this town,
There's no room for clumps and grains,
Or waves who stir up the ocean brown,
Or ripples and surges and disturbances.

To the clumps and grains, they say,
"Stay settled at the bottom,
Out of sight and out of mind!
Why did you, sediment, never dissolve?"
I've wondered this from time to time.

And that little Panic torments us
With her daily journey to the shore.
Not a single of us in this town
Have ever casted her a lure,
And yet still she comes routinely.

What a tiring job it is indeed
To squeeze down each and every swell,
And without my steady wrangling,
We know very well
That dear Joy would hit the road.

On occasion, Panic brings a wave
That is far too big for me,
And Joy leaves town for far too long
(For certain storms are known to level cities).
Lately the water is remaining murky,
And I know Panic is somewhere there, lurking.

It might be time to cast some bait
And sit her down for a nice long talk,
And request that Joy listen
To see if they could ever get along.

Maybe then Joy and Panic
Will know that they both belong,
And I will sit on the bank with them
And forget that anything was ever wrong.

Mirage

To live requires a holding
Under the magnifying glass.
Look at your reflection...
Are you not a machine built for alchemy?

Are we not clusters of the elements,
Which pull themselves in and transform,
Kneading themselves into a temporary bread?

Are we not like a serpent digesting its prey,
With each swallow metabolizing,
Leading itself to the final expulsion?

The more you decompose
Particular perception,
All distinction dissolves into one.

And when our breath returns to the wind,
And our waters join the ocean,
And our matter finds its home in the soil,
And our temperature matches the greater room,
It is the breaking down of a cluster,
The release of a holding, a blockage,
Like the One just got knotted up for a bit,
And the kink was worked out in the end.

So we are both life and food for life,
A living thing and a hologram.
A planet and a speck on the telescope's lens.
A mirage and a lagoon up ahead.
Like a phantom pool,
We dance along the damp and warm places
Where the air meets the earth,
Animated on the horizon of perception.

Acknowledgments

My deepest, most heartfelt gratitude goes to my family and friends for their support and encouragement. To my Mom (Amy) and Dad (John), Step-Mom (Olga) and Step-Dad (Vic), to my grandparents and extended loved ones, of blood or otherwise: You have all been influential in the making of this book. In times of trouble, we realize who and what is most important. I hope to never take that for granted.

To my partner, Rob, who is my loving muse and ardent supporter, I hope to continue writing love poems about you and making memories that spark the creative fire within us with such fierceness and fearlessness. A soft place to land has become a true home, a place to heal, a place to love, and a place to create. Thank you for shining your light. You mean the world to me.

A special thanks goes to Jennifer Bright, Bright Communications, and the team who contributed so generously to this project. You are the fairy godmothers of books and have helped bring to life what I thought was only a dream. You are doing such important work.

Lastly, I'd like to thank the self (mine and yours). I'm grateful that I have bravely trusted and honored the messages that have come through me, and I am ever so grateful to you, the reader, for being a mirror, a witness, and a supporter of poetry, art, and the things that require a slower pace and a little dash of attention in an increasingly swift and stimulating world.

Thank you.

About the Author

Anna Camryn Wilde is a writer and entrepreneur based in the Pocono Mountains of Pennsylvania. From a young age, Anna was an avid reader who took an interest in philosophy, literature, psychology, mysticism, and the natural world. After completing her B.A. in English with a minor in psychology, she has professionally written for the health and wellness field for the last seven years, with topics ranging from Ayurvedic supplements to psychedelic therapy. She integrates her creative passions, adoration for nature, and boundless curiosity through her writing.